Rory Church

Black Lyon Publishing, LLC

HOLD ME AGAIN
Copyright © 2015 by Keith Zwingelberg

Our books may be ordered through your local bookstore or by
visiting the publisher:

BlackLyonPublishing.com

Black Lyon Publishing, LLC
PO Box 567
Baker City, OR 97814

This is a work of fiction. All of the characters, names, events,
organizations and conversations in this novel are either the products
of the author's vivid imagination or are used in a fictitious way for the
purposes of this story.

ISBN-13: 978-1-934912-72-0
Library of Congress Control Number: 2015904554

Published and printed in
the United States of America.

Black Lyon Contemporary Romance

For Monica Morse.

Acknowledgement:

The author would like to thank his critically accurate editor Susan Mary Malone, Beta readers Diane Heikkinen and his wife Gwenn, as well as the Black Lyon Publishing staff. He would also like to express his undying gratitude to the members of the American Armed Forces and our country's first responders. Freedom is not Free.

Chapter 1

Emergency Room
Palmer, South Dakota

Rotating tunnels of drifting snow whipped off the icy ramp as a dual-wheeled ambulance picked its way up the slippery slope from the emergency room. Tracy's head snapped quickly to movement out the corner of her eye, senses honed in the villages of Afghanistan—attacking insurgents. "Get down!" she yelled, pushing Old Sam, the scraggly Indian orderly, behind the reception desk. She reached under her scrubs for her Beretta before realizing neither existed ... the insurgents nor her sidearm.

A faded, square-bodied F-150 pickup truck, brakes squealing, careened down the frozen ramp. The entry door's electronic motion-sensors, detecting movement, noiselessly attempted to slide open.

Fishtailing, the truck clipped the side of the ambulance and thunderously ricocheted into the narrow gap of the opening doors. The glass panels jumped off their tracks, miraculously not shattering. The farm truck screeched to a halt, hood and headlight on the passenger side pinned halfway into the emergency room.

Tracy's heart pounded in her ears as the distinct odor of hot engine oil assaulted her.

What the hell?

A frigid gust scattered papers off counters as the driver, in an orange hunter's cap, clambered from behind the steering wheel. Clad in a dark blue vest, jeans, and work boots he vaulted onto the hood of the vehicle, leather-gloved hands trying futilely to pry open the broken door.

"It's stuck. Damn it!"

The driver's straining features and sunburned face scowled at Tracy. Blond curls poked from under his cap, and the palest of blue eyes riveted her. Jake Moran. The man who had plagued her dreams the past ten years, and the man who nearly took her virginity.

Jake peered through the gap into the largely empty medical facility. "We're gonna need a lot of help out here … right now." Dilated pupils declared his urgency. "Somebody has shot Stephen Kincaid."

•

The burning in Jake's lungs eased and his heartbeat slowed. He'd made it to the hospital and not crashed through the glass entrance of the emergency room. Maybe, just maybe, the doctors and nurses could save the Kincaid kid.

What a mess, and with the damn freezing, Canadian storm closing in on the Black Hills. He'd been up early in the morning with Duke, his shepherd-lab mix, trying to get one last survey of his ranch fences before snowdrifts covered them for the winter. He'd found the Kincaid kid lying just north of the ranch's fence line behind the rock outcropping that marked the trailhead to Horse Thief Ridge—a bullet hole in his chest and half his shoulder blade blown away.

"Oh my God! Geez … What happened?" A nurse in Christmas scrubs stood beside the truck bed, pulling a stethoscope from around her neck and staring at the blood-covered horse blanket.

Jake jumped off the hood of the truck, realizing she'd come out the side door.

"Get a gurney out here—STAT!" the nurse hollered back through the open door. "And call a trauma alert. This is real bad. We're going to need a surgeon."

A young girl with telemetry headphones scrambled about retrieving papers that had blown throughout the waiting room. A stooped grey-haired Indian, also in scrubs, pushed a white sheet-covered gurney down the hall in front of the reception desk. Jake helped him maneuver the gurney through the pedestrian entrance door.

"I said what happened?" the nurse yelled as she jumped up into the bed of the snow, and dirt-covered truck. She removed the rigid, frozen blanket from around the kid. "How long's he been down? Did you find him like this? My God … it is Stephen!"

Duke, tail wagging excitedly, paced back and forth in the cab of the truck.

Blood pumped in Jake's temples as he tried to give the agile woman the information she demanded. Everything seemed to move at lightning speed, except the nurse who calmly and methodically assessed the dying boy.

She paid little attention to Jake's pause for recollection or the gnawing, swirling wind that whipped the snow from the bed of his truck. Her full lips moved deliberately as she questioned him while her hands deftly lifted the boy's eyelids and settled briefly on the side of his neck, checking for a pulse.

"Okay … can you grab his feet, Jake? Help us get him on the gurney." She positioned herself with hands under the boy's shoulders, supporting his head.

Dark hair hung down obscuring her face but not the soft smooth skin at the angle of her jaw. There was a familiarity to the set of her mouth and the flip of her bangs.

"Yeah, sure." He looked around. Where was everyone?

"He's not that heavy," the nurse said. "On three let's move him. One, two, three."

Jake and the efficient nurse easily slid the still body onto the gurney held steady by the old Indian. Bloodied rags fell onto the ice and salt at the emergency room entrance. Kincaid had made a moan when Jake first lifted him, nothing this time. And it didn't look like he was breathing.

"I found him up by Boxelder Gulch," Jake said, finally getting his mind in gear. He followed them through the emergency receiving area toward a trauma room. What the heck! The whole place looked deserted.

"Gunshot wound!" the nurse shouted.

"He hit his head too, it looks like," Jake said. "Probably when he fell."

The nurse moved a stethoscope calculatingly about the bloodied chest. "Get Dr. Morsette. This will need to be explored. Oh hell, there's blood everywhere." She pulled the stethoscope from her ears. "And call a Code Blue. He isn't breathing and there's no pulse. Precordial rate is fifteen to twenty ... We're losing him!"

The reception clerk, mouth agape, dumped an armful of papers behind the counter, hit a red button on the wall, and punched numbers on a phone.

Repeatedly, a soft yet distinct tone echoed through the hospital. Jake pushed the handle of the sink next to the reception desk with his elbow, and washed his bloody cold hands. The warm water felt good, but stung. He tried to remember the Kincaids' phone number, but was unsure if it ended in a two or a five.

He glanced down the deserted hallway while he wiped dried blood from between his fingers. Green garland hung from the ceiling with interspersed red and silver Christmas bells. Where was everyone and how did the nurse know him?

Chapter 2

Trauma Bay, Patriot's Hospital Emergency Room

Wiry Sam Whitcomb pumped on the Kincaid kid's chest. Between compressions, Tracy cut off the stained and soiled shirt. Blood spray emanated from the open chest wound but no frank hemorrhaging—not a good sign. When they stopped bleeding, they died. That, she'd learned in Afghanistan.

She placed a sterile chuck pad over the obvious entrance wound and checked for a carotid pulse with the chest compressions. The work of the resuscitation sent a burning up her back and amplified the sinking turn her stomach had taken at the dire condition of Stephen Kincaid ... and the unexpected appearance of Jake Moran.

The hospital nursing supervisor and a young respiratory therapist arrived with a flourish of charts and equipment. The slim, blond-haired girl—who looked like a high school kid—tucked her pony tail into a surgical cap and, with a brightly lighted laryngoscope, expertly slipped a tube into the boy's trachea. After attaching a breath analyzer and listening with a stethoscope, she nodded.

Tracy sensed the tall and lanky Jake standing near the door to the trauma room. She tightened a tourniquet around the pale arm hanging off the gurney and grabbed a large-bore plastic-shrouded needle for intravenous access. While threading the catheter into the crook of the Kincaid kid's arm, she shouted across the maelstrom to the records clerk holding a clipboard, "He's bleeding out! Alexis, get to the blood bank and bring back two handfuls of O blood. Don't let anyone stop you. I need you back in five minutes tops!"

From the far corner of the room, the mousy clerk dumped the

clipboard and pen on top of the crash cart and slid out the door.

Tracy hollered after her, "If they want blood samples and bands, have them come back with you!" She glanced at Jake. In the sky-blue of his eyes she perceived the faintest glimmer of recognition.

She flicked her head at the discarded clipboard. "Can you jot down the times and medications as best you can … We're a little shorthanded right now."

Jake stared at the busy medical team and then grimaced at his still dirty hands.

"Sink's over there and gloves are on the outside of the door." She indicated with her shoulder as she placed a clear dressing over the 16-gauge intravenous catheter and secured it with four pieces of tape. "We've got access—" She looked at Jake. "Zero eight forty-three. Just start at the top and write the times and anything you hear being done, or meds given."

He began writing.

Emergency cart doors opened and clanked closed with regularity and murmured reports of completed tasks filtered through the occasional barked order as the crew worked through the preset trauma sequence.

The Monday morning crew was shorthanded. The Packers' fault. In fact it wasn't even Tracy's shift this morning. The Sunday night game had gone into overtime, and here she was covering for Carl, the hung-over emergency charge nurse. His early morning rambling text had been followed by a pleading cell phone call. Apparently the Packers had lost—or given the game away. She understood their frustration but really, being a Minnesota Vikings fan like her dad, she couldn't care less about the lackluster Packers.

Well, Carl was the free soul who'd taken a leap of faith the previous summer and hired her fresh out of the Navy. Four years at dispensaries and two tours on the ground in Helmand Province, all with the Marines.

Thank God she was back home. She'd actually slept through the night a couple of times this week without sedatives. After a few months out of the war zone, normalization of sleep should occur. At least that was what the doctors and debriefing manuals said. *God let that be me*—not one of the stressed-out veterans who could never sleep again without heavy doses of medications.

The first few weeks back had her wondering. Bloody bodies and missing legs continually appeared in her dreams—nightmares. Call them what they were—Post-Traumatic Stress. Not a disorder, yet. Still, why had she, Lieutenant Tracy Aspen, survived? Why did she get to come home with all her limbs intact? Was it the act of a protecting God or just simply fate ... or beating the odds?

•

Multiple simultaneous resuscitation tasks happened quickly. The adolescent respiratory therapist competently reported no breath sounds on the left. The nursing supervisor, Hillary Post, snapped orders for defibrillator paddles and epinephrine. Blood arrived the same time as the general surgeon, Doctor Morsette, who concentrated first on the collapsed lung.

After filling six blood vials, Tracy glanced up to a muscular Jake Moran, complete with plastic gown and gloves, having replaced Sam Whitcomb on cardiac compressions. She supposed he'd received CPR training during his time with the National Park Service.

A blur of blood bags and medication syringes flew around the trauma room.

"Stop spiking any more blood." Doctor Roger Morsette stepped back and removed his gloves. "Hold CPR ... note time of death at zero nine twenty-seven."

They had been working on the basically lifeless form of Steven Kincaid for nearly three-quarters of an hour. It felt like mere minutes. The nursing supervisor had taken over chest compressions from Jake at some point. Now she removed bloodied pink gloves from the Kincaid kid's chest and climbed off the step stool she'd used to get better chest compressions. The therapist and surgeon had controlled the boy's respirations but even epinephrine and cardiac shocks failed to return any heart rhythm. He was dead.

A real lousy start to the day.

The trauma room at once transformed from a noisy medical factory to the hushed tranquility of a tomb. Orderlies and therapists quietly retrieved their instruments and equipment. What talking occurred was soft and whispered, in reverence for the recently deceased.

Tracy pulled a sheet over the body as Hillary and Sam Whitcomb put needles in red plastic containers and soiled gauze and towels in a red trash bag. She pulled the cut-open coat and denim shirt from beneath the body. Tucked in an inside coat pocket she found a bloodied peacock feather. The futility struck her as did a pang of ancient Indian teaching. She placed the feather in the bag with Kincaid's personal effects. Maybe it was an Indian thing, but feathers had significances in other religions, too.

Mustached Sheriff Brad Schaffer sat in the hallway facing Jake, his right butt cheek perched precariously on a clean gurney. In his large, sun-weathered hand he held a small notebook that he gestured with every few moments. Jake had removed the blue examination gloves, however, the blood-spattered white plastic gown still hung from his neck. It had been nearly a decade since she'd literally gone for a tumble in the hay with the high school quarterback. He hadn't remembered her.

Tracy had spent the years away at nursing school in Arizona and at Marine dispensaries or medevac hospitals in Afghanistan. She knew in October, when she'd come back to the Dakotas, that Jake Moran still lived and worked in Palmer. An injured football player, Jake had been dumped by his socialite girlfriend his senior year of high school. Tracy had caught him on the rebound. And with open blouse and unbuttoned Levis, she'd nearly lost her virginity until an aroused and red-faced Jake pulled back and asked her that fateful question.

"Just how old are you?"

He apparently didn't like her answer, even though she'd added a half-year. Her skinny hips and small breasts probably did little to convince him of her maturity. She'd long ago gotten over that school-girl crush … at least she thought she had until this morning. The Sheriff gave Tracy a half-smile and used the notebook to tip an imaginary hat to her. The real hat, a law enforcement khaki Stetson, sat next to him.

"Sheriff." She nodded, turned, and walked to the large metal sink against the hallway wall, and kneed the automatic wash sequence.

He continued his interview with Jake. "So how long you reckon he was down when you found him?"

"Couldn't have been long. He'd bled a lot, though."

The Sheriff shifted his weight, a tight set to his mouth. "Was

Stephen part of the militia?"

Jake glared at the Sheriff and shook his head, disgusted. "I don't know, Sheriff ... Let's not get going in that direction."

"You got a rifle in your truck?" The Sheriff pounded the note pad on his palm as he studied Jake. "You know I haven't seen the Kincaid kid around much lately."

Jake's eyes burned a hole in the Sheriff. "You're welcome to check my rifle out anytime ... As for Stephen, I've heard he was up in Toronto going to school or working, just got home for the holidays." He exhaled slowly and twisted his neck with an audible crack. "We done here, Sheriff?"

Jake glanced over at Tracy, biting his lower lip. He still didn't recognize her. Yet he stared at her longer than someone normally did. Certainly the heat of the situation, with the killing and all, probably made it hard to dredge up old memories, especially when the Sheriff had him backed against the wall, grilling him on the morning's events.

She extended a well-washed hand to the Sheriff. "I'm Tracy Aspen. I just got back in town a few weeks back. Sorry to meet under these circumstances."

Jake nodded and a slight smile creased his full lips. The twinkle of his blue eyes illuminated a bit more dramatically. Maybe it did, or maybe the reflection off the emergency room window created the illusion.

Tracy shook her head. "He didn't make it. Doctor Morsette just pronounced him. Really, we did everything we could under the circumstances." She shifted her gaze from the Sheriff to Jake.

The smiling lips were now tight and he continued to nibble on the lower one.

"Honestly, he didn't have much of a chance from the start, to tell you the truth," she said. Being a nurse and ex-military, unfortunately, prepared her some for the death of young men. Her heart tugged though, at the emotion pent up inside Jake. But there was more than just sorrow in his demeanor. He was angry.

Jake stood looking down and massaging his forehead. "It ... it didn't look good out at the ranch. I—"

"You did everything you could've, as best I can tell," the Sheriff said. "Like you said, it could be a huntin' accident. But we need to treat it like a crime scene ... until we make a determination."

Tracy asked the Sheriff, "You think it was intentional?" She knew the answer. She glanced at Jake and back to the Sheriff. "Yeah, I guess one shot to the mid-chest is not likely an accident. Looks like the sniper shots our soldiers took in the Gulf."

"Right, probably not an accident." The Sheriff closed his note book and buttoned it into his shirt pocket. "I'll need you to ride with me out to your ranch, Jake. Leave your truck here for now so the crime scene people can run through it."

Jake's shoulder noticeably tightened as he marched up the hall-way to a trash can. He carefully pulled the straps of the bloody white gown over his head. "I need to let the Kincaids know about Stephen ... They might be expecting him home sometime this morning." When he turned back there was a tight set to his jaw.

"Nah, I think it's best if you leave the notification to us," the Sheriff said. "They're probably not involved but we do need to see their response and get statements." He frowned under Jake's glar-ing eyes. "I know ... it sucks. It always sucks." The Sheriff slid off the gurney and lumbered over to Hillary and Alexis who were double-checking times, medications, and defibrillation attempts. Tracy heard something about time-of-death mumbled.

The chill down her spine blended with the light breeze that in-termittently gusted through the broken entry doors. An inch or more of fine, new snow covered the roof of Jake's truck.

Aunt Clair's ex-husband had been a member of the Wyoming Militia back during the Reagan years. He'd spent five years in the federal prison at Sheridan for possession of automatic weapons and apparently bomb-making. Tracy's mother, Clair's older sister, helped get the family back on their feet over near Bismarck.

"You stay away from those militia idiots," had been her mother's admonition to Tracy and her brothers anytime the discussion had come up.

As she watched the storm clouds race in from the north, an im-age reflected off the icy glass door.

"Little Tracy Aspen all grown up."

She turned to face Jake, arms folded across her chest.

"Sorry to ruin your mornin'," he said, rolling up wet shirt sleeves from where he'd washed at the scrub sink—the stiffness now out of his stance.

"Right ... Not so good for you either. And it looks like the Sheriff isn't through with you." She stared up into the handsomely weathered face, etched a bit from the morning's events.

He nodded.

Her heart fluttered and a warm glow rose in her chest. She was over the school-girl crush. Still, a restless drumming deep in her core whispered for attention.

In high school she'd confided to her mother her strong attraction to Jake. The peculiar smile on her mother's face as she brushed a straggling bang of hair behind Tracy's ear had haunted her all these years. As it turned out, Jake hooked back up with his steady, Natalie, shortly after he'd rejected her in the barn. Had her mother also lost her first love?

Sam Whitcomb, red trash bags held in tanned gnarled hands, paused next to them and squinted out through the frosty glass door. "We gonna be in for it, not too long."

"Before the week's end," Tracy said. "If the weather scans are right."

"A regular ol' Alberta Clipper." Whitcomb set one bag down and pushed scraggly grey hair behind his ear. "Hope they know 'bout it up on the reservation … Lost nine people back in '62."

"I haven't heard it called that in years." Sparks danced in Jake's eyes as he gazed out at the darkening clouds. "They say there's a warm, moist front moving up from the south, too. We're in for a real load of snow I'm afraid."

Whitcomb ambled with the trash bags to the back of the emergency room as the Sheriff approached Jake. The Indian mumbled back over his shoulder, "I think so. The Park lost a bunch of buffalo in '62 also … It could be hard."

"What's he takin' about?" the Sheriff asked. "That Canadian storm movin' in?"

Tracy smiled. "It's probably my fault. I've been praying for a white Christmas for over six months … sorry."

•

Jake stood at the base of the ambulance ramp, therapeutically petting Duke and letting the tension ease from his muscles. Lazy snowflakes peppered his and Duke's heads as the fragrance of Ponderosa Pine gusted from the west. Across the parking lot, a Santa

Claus lumbered out of his car and hefted a large bag of presents over his shoulder before heading to the main hospital entrance.

The changes in Tracy Aspen had weakened Jake's knees. Lord, the penetrating maturity of her eyes and the soft beauty of her bronzed skin—he'd wanted to reach out and stroke her cheek. His breath caught as he remembered how close he'd come to ravaging her in the hay loft so many years back. How different would his life have been if he'd kept going? Couldn't be worse ... could it?

Earlier, the morning had been serene and picturesque. Cold for sure, but fresh mountain air the likes of which nearly half the world had never breathed. Sunshine crested the blue-green ridge beyond the barn as he'd finished pulling feed down from the loft. The mixed taste of dry hay and musty cattle stuck in his throat despite the bandana across his nose and mouth. Cattle groaned and mooed at him, warning him that as sure as the sun was rising, the winter was also descending on the Lazy T.

A glance toward the state road and back toward Horse Thief Ridge had confirmed that he was alone on the six-hundred-acre ranch. Before he left the barn he rechecked the 9mm Smith and Wesson under the hay next to the pitchfork and the 12-gauge shotgun in a panel next to the massive, sliding, double door. A habit he'd developed out of independent necessity. It had been over a year since he'd detected any incursion into his personal life. Were the federal authorities leaving him alone finally or just being more successful at hiding their activities?

As much as the scent of musty cattle had settled the tightness in his chest he still had not shaken the suspicions and mistrust of the past few years, unfounded accusations that had cost him his career as a Park Service Ranger. How? He wasn't sure, but as unquestionable as the approaching snow storm—someone had set him up.

Certainly his mom and kid sister would help any way they could, but the hole he'd been dug into was way over their heads. They had absolutely tried, showing up at the ranch on birthdays and holidays. His sister, Catherine, had made several efforts to get him back to church. It wasn't like he didn't believe and all. He just was not ready for the town folks' moral scrutiny. He had only himself, Duke and the ranch to rely on ... that is where his future lay.

He'd shipped forty-three yearlings off to the feed lot in Rapid City the month before. Money in the bank to cover the mortgage and a little extra for some needed improvements on the worn-down ranch. A few supply runs up to the North Dakota oil fields this winter might feather his nest-egg even more.

Today had been dedicated to surveying the fences and getting together an estimate of supplies for the spring. Clouds to the north and west had emerged from the dawn sky as he'd ushered Duke into the aging truck and bumped up the frozen pasture road, quietly appreciating the new day. The far-off echoes of rifle shots bouncing off rocky pinnacles and the pine-covered cliffs announced hunters, out for the last elk or deer of the season before deep drifts of snow made hunting impossible.

The trail to Horse Thief Ridge paralleled the ranch property for nearly a quarter mile before cutting abruptly through Boxelder Gulch to a steep ascent up the backside of Mount Rushmore. Though not an official trail, it was used by local hunters and had probably been an Indian footpath for centuries.

He'd found the Kincaid kid laying with his left arm tucked under a torso covered in blood, his right arm bent awkwardly between two rocks. Unconscious—and with a fist-sized bloodied hole torn in his coat. Bile had risen in Jake's mouth and still as he thought of the scene he struggled to swallow against the dryness in his throat. At six-two and a former football player, Jake had easily hefted the skinny kid into the back of his truck. Duke nervously paced across the seat of the truck intermittently barking instructions or encouragement. A bundle of rags stuffed into the shoulder blade helped slow the bleeding. The horse blanket off his saddle, in the bed of the truck, had to do for the cold, rough trip into town.

Jake had just begun to settle into a natural rhythm with the ranch, had finally come to grips with the events of the past two years. Would it start up again? The allegations of his association with the Wyoming Militia, home-grown survivalist terrorists—many were sons and grandsons of Wyoming homesteaders—and some were his friends from college. The charges weren't true. Sure he understood where the independent-minded ranchers and self-reliant patriots were coming from. But violence was crazy. So why had he been singled out?

A light crunching of snow behind him and the perking of Duke's ears brought Jake back to the present, violent morning. Tracy, wrapped in a white cotton hospital blanket, stood closed-lipped three paces behind him.

"He won't bite," Jake said.

Duke's brow creased considering the strange figure approaching them.

"Duke, good boy."

The dog's right ear twitched but his eyes never left Tracy.

She knelt and offered the back of her hand. "Hey Duke ... You make friends easily?"

"He's a pushover for women." Jake smirked. "Most women anyway." Duke had never warmed to Natalie or vice versa. That probably should have told him something.

Two sniffs and Duke accepted a tentative pet on the head from Tracy—a quick judge of character—Jake had never known the dog to be wrong.

"There you are," Sheriff Schaffer hollered from behind Jake's truck. "Ready to hit the road?"

"I'll need to drop the dog at my mom's house on the way out ... It's just off Main."

"Long as he don't have fleas," the Sheriff said.

No one else noticed but Jake detected a slight raise of the hairy cackles on Duke's neck.

Tracy squeezed Jake's elbow gently. "Pop in and have a cup of coffee with me when you come back for your truck."

He sensed her nursing composure—caring and compassionate—a world of difference from the spindly legged girl from high school. "Yeah, that would be great." His stomach did a quick flip. It probably would help to talk with someone besides Duke.

Chapter 3

Outside Palmer

State highway 244 was usually a modern thoroughfare, a highly traveled tourist route through the attraction-laden Black Hills. Today though, it consisted of a series of lazy white curves winding through rock outcroppings. Snow accented holly fern and burdock interspersed among steep banks of pine and aspen. Gusting wind bent and rustled the tree tops, yet near the ground only the occasional swirl of snow interrupted the magical white blanket.

Sheriff Schaffer squinted through the windshield wipers. "We might have one hell of a time finding anything with this snow comin' in." The fine snow flurries had given way to sluggish feathery flakes.

"You'll need to lock in your four-wheel drive to get up the north pasture road," Jake said as they approached the turn out to the Lazy T.

The Sheriff nodded. "It don't make no sense. Who would want to shoot that scrawny Kincaid kid?"

Jake kept his mouth shut firmly as he climbed out of the front cab. He was not going to give the law a single reason to start rummaging through his life again. Blowing snow covered his footprints nearly immediately after each step he took to the south pasture fence line.

He re-latched the simple gate, stood next to the Sheriff's window and pointed toward a low row of buildings in the distance, silhouetted against the swirling snow. "You gotta take it slow so you don't throw an axle on some of those frozen ruts."

Seen from this vantage, Jake grudgingly conceded that life on a remote South Dakota ranch was a lonely, solitary lifestyle that was unlikely to change for him anytime soon.

They eased behind the old ranch house hugging a track close to the rundown fence. Up ahead, a half mile or so, a blue-gray rock face materialized through the flurries. Young Deputy Caulfield sat behind Jake. The wiry law enforcement officer anxiously rechecked his service revolver for the second time since they'd left the main road.

Jake glanced at the burly Sheriff, who nodded his understanding.

"You miss being a Ranger?" the Sheriff asked, changing the subject.

"Not on days like today." Jake snorted and gazed up at the rough crags of the Black Hills as they bounced up to a fence line. "If he was shot, it was likely from up on that crest." He pointed to an area where the snow-covered treeline became intermittent with spires of projecting rock. The ancient Lakota of the area called them needles of the gods.

"It's been at least four hours now," Schaffer said. "Any shooter is probably long gone."

"Who the hell would want to shoot Stephen?" Jake shook his head as the heat in the vehicle gradually crept back into his shoulders and sore right leg.

"Could'a been mistaken identity," Caulfield said from the back seat.

"There are a dozen ways up and down from that ridge." Jake turned and glanced toward the rifle rack on the back window of the crew cab truck. "I'd have a scope on that crest while we're poking around down here."

At a nod from the Sheriff, the deputy removed the 300 Winchester and, fumbling a bit, chambered three rounds.

"We're not hunting, Clay. Fill the damn chamber." The Sheriff shifted his two-hundred-plus fireplug frame about the driver's seat of the truck. He pointed to the spot he wanted covered as the truck came to a stop. "Forensics radioed back at the gate … said your rifle is cleared."

Jake glanced into the gulch and up the ridgeline above. Buckthorn and mullein scrubs moved lazily in the gulch but up on the ridgeline the trees, shrouded in clouds, bent against the wind.

"Did you really think I'd shoot my neighbor's kid?"

The Sheriff nodded to the deputy. "Clay, get your eyes on that ridge."

The deputy zipped up his jacket and pulled his hat down tight on his head as snow flurries swirled in through the back door.

Once the door was closed, the Sheriff turned to Jake. "Look, I never bought into that crap about you and the militia. But my job is to check every possibility." He pulled at stubble on his chin. "You've been keeping pretty quiet out here the past year or so. Best to stay with that plan I'd say."

"Right," Jake said. He and his family had known Schaffer for over thirty years. Jake trusted him as much as he could trust any law enforcement officer. But someone had marked him and maybe it was a coordinated effort. Best just to play his cards close the chest and see what developed.

"How far up the trail did you find him?" the Sheriff asked.

"Right at the start," Jake said. "Whoever shot him likely waited for him to show up."

"It would seem that way." Schaffer leaned on the steering wheel and frowned up the rocky slope of Horse Thief Ridge. "You ever run into this when you were rangering?"

Jake eased out and positioned the truck between himself and the cloud-covered rim barely visible through the snow flurries. He popped his neck, relieving the tension that had settled in. "I've dealt with a couple bands of poachers out of Montana. No one got killed, but a ranger and a couple of poachers were shot."

"I remember that," the Sheriff said as he eased out of the truck.

The deputy braced his left elbow on the hood, fixed his eye to the rifle site, and swung an arch back and forth, a little too quickly, across the shadow covered ridgeline.

"You involved much?" the Sheriff asked.

"I got a piece of one of their asses when they nearly killed Gene Bearclaw." Jake shifted his gaze along the outcroppings high above.

"The Lakota-Sioux?"

"Right. Grazed his right chest ... and it did drop his lung. Touch and go for awhile." Jake gave one more look to the far ends of the ridge, zipped his vest up to the neck, and pulled on leather work gloves. "They're rotting in Yuma Federal Prison now."

"All clear, Sheriff," the deputy said, readjusting the cowboy hat on his brown crew-cut scalp.

"I imagine the shooting happened before this weather moved in." The Sheriff held the barbwire fence apart for Jake to crawl through. He reciprocated on the other side.

"You know," Jake said. "I do remember hearing some rifle shots early when I was getting hay out of the loft ... before I headed up to the pasture. Figured it was hunters out for the last of the season."

"Before sunup?" the Sheriff asked.

"Hard to tell with the clouds and all," Jake scratched behind his ear. "But probably right before sunup ... It wasn't still dark out. I know that."

A rolling plain of needle grass and sagebrush ran to the north-west, sinking into the dry-sand and rock-strewn gulch, silently being covered by deepening snow. A hundred yards from the arroyo, the sand gave way to a boulder- and rock-covered sheer cliff. The morning flurry had painted a mosaic across the high bank like a sugar-dusted pastry. Fast-moving weather raced from peaks to crest lines over the Black Hills, leaving the ridge nearly invisible behind a low line of clouds.

Jake crouched near the boulders and pointed to where he'd found young Kincaid. He tried to spit into the dirt but the saliva in his mouth felt like molasses.

Scattered blotches and specks of blood stained the rocks. Over the next half hour, the law enforcement officers circled out from the crime scene as threatening snow clouds to the north continued to grow. They found no tracks, ground disruptions, or suspicious objects that would help the Sheriff in his investigation. Nothing.

The Sheriff stood from examining the ground. "We're gonna have to go up on that rim if we hope to find any evidence." Drifting and blowing snow had already started to cover the boulders at the trail head.

"I really haven't been up there much," Jake said. "The ridge and both sides of it are privately owned." The blanket of snow accumulating on the pines near the crest was nearly continuous now. "The temperature up there must be dropping pretty fast ... Snow's starting to stick." A sinking sensation gnawed at his stomach.

"I don't think the national park land starts till just this side of the monument," the Sheriff said. "Is that right?"

"Yeah." Jake took a step back and pulled at his lower lip. "Park starts to the east, the next ridge over." He glanced up briefly then rubbed his fingers across his three-day-old beard.

"Right," the Sheriff said. He slapped his snow-covered hat against his thigh. "Park Service crap, sorry."

The muscles at the base of Jake's neck tighten and his injured football knee throbbed with cold and anticipation. "Water over the dam, Sheriff."

The bitterness of Jake's dismissal from the Park Service three years earlier had been diluted by his severance pay. Cash he'd used as a down payment on the two-hundred-forty-acre Lazy T Ranch just outside Palmer, the reinvention of a childhood dream. Jake had grown up at the twenty-thousand-acre Circle R Ranch, where his mother ran the kitchen. The owners, the Reynolds, had given him the run of the ranch and treated him like a grandchild following his father's accidental death. Ranching had been his father's dream and it was in Jake's blood as well.

His mother and Catherine now ran a successful café in Palmer, the Mountain Rose.

He grimaced at the Sheriff. "Besides, I'd still be digging fire lines today instead of shoveling out my own barn."

"Frozen manure before too long." The Sheriff rested his hand on Jake's shoulder. "We still need to git up to that ledge, and soon."

"I don't think I can help you much with the trails up there, Sheriff," Jake said and looked over at Clay Caulfield.

"Hey, don't look at me. My sport is whitewater kayaking." The deputy began ejecting rifle rounds as they all climbed back into the truck.

Jake glanced back to the complex of sheds, barn, and framed house that made up his ranch. Blowing snow highlighted the loneliness of the cattleman's life he'd embraced. His heart tugged at a fleeting vision of his family sitting before a crackling fireplace at the Circle R ranch, so many years ago. Family—a wife and children of his own—it hadn't been the right time yet. He hadn't even made a serious run at a woman in nearly two years. Maybe that needed to change.

•

The Sheriff sat with both hands resting atop the steering

wheel.

He scrunched his nose and scowled at Jake. "I need to talk with the Kincaids."

"There's a ranch road that cuts across the bottomlands beyond the west fence line," Jake said. "It's a little soft going through the gulch, but your four-wheel should be fine."

"You're serious. You want to be there when I tell 'em?"

Jake's stomach turned over. Death had always crept up on him unexpectedly. First his father's accident when he was young. Largely he'd been ignored, with all the rush of attempted emergency medical care and then the anguish of his mother and Catherine. They had been tearful and questioning. Lamenting why had God let this happen? Their family friends and the church had spent hours and days at his mother's and sister's sides. All Jake got was an occasional firm hand on the shoulder and, "You're the man of the family now."

It was his first real brush with mortality and he suffered through it alone and silent.

The death of Bret Peterson, equally unexpected, had propelled him into a legal and departmental review that he still did not totally understand. Apparently Peterson was in the Black Hills on an undercover assignment. At least that was the best Jake could discern. Why he had been so ferociously implicated in the Ranger's death and where the information incriminating him had come from was "classified." The Park Service was sorry, but sacrifices had to be made—whatever that meant.

Who had killed Stephen Kincaid and why? It was not his job. He was not in law enforcement anymore. But the Kincaids were neighbors and they deserved any answers he could provide. Jake swallowed hard. "You going now?" he asked the Sheriff.

"I will. But you got to promise to keep your mouth shut. You just tell them what I ask you to tell 'em. They ask any question ... I answer them." He held Jake's stare. "You got it, rancher?"

Jake rubbed his hands in front of the dash heater and nodded. He wasn't interested in getting grilled or second guessed like had happened in the Peterson investigation. He would just as soon keep his mouth shut. He just needed to be there for Clint and Margret Kincaid. Not that he wanted to be, but it's what you did in South Dakota. He exhaled slowly through his nose trying to keep the tightness out of his shoulders.

The combination of northern latitude, short winter days and darkening clouds produced a false dusk as they powered across Boxelder Gulch. Even though it was not yet three o'clock the kitchen and family room lights were on in the Kincaid house.

Pine and juniper shrubs dotted the landscape as they emerged from the Kincaids' east pasture behind a metal pole barn. Near the house a snow-dusted mature white spruce covered in twinkling dark blue Christmas lights guarded a large wooden porch that ran across most of the front of the ranch-style home. To the north and behind the stucco and wood mid-80s house, a stand of aspen spread out over nearly an acre wrapping around to the west, the slender, leafless branches reaching to a dull grey sky.

Inside the house two dogs yelped as the Sheriff eased his truck into the ranch yard. The porch light came on and Clint Kincaid stepped out onto the porch. A Minnesota Vikings flag hung from the roof post.

"Schaffer." Clint stood on the porch but made no effort to approach the Sheriff's vehicle.

"Clint." The two men nearly the same age probably had known each other for over half a century. The Sheriff made no attempt to talk to Clint Kincaid until he was up on the porch.

Caulfield stood next to the truck, but Jake followed the Sheriff and stopped at the bottom of the stairs. Margret Kincaid peeked through the stained glass side panel of the front door.

"Clint," the Sheriff repeated and tipped his hat toward Mrs. Kincaid. "We've come about Stephen."

The tanned, leathery skin on Clint Kincaid's face faded to a morbid grey. His jaw slacked.

Through the door, the nearly deaf Margret boomed. "What did he say, Clint?" The door opened and as she wiped her hands on an apron, she turned what must have been her best ear toward the Sheriff.

Clint Kincaid glared at his wife and without raising his voice mouthed. "They came about Stephen."

Her hands went to her mouth. "Is he all right? He's been very sick … Hasn't been home all day."

"Left early this mornin'," Clint said. "Is he in trouble?"

"He's dead, Clint." The Sheriff sure didn't beat around the

bush.

Margret Kincaid understood the Sheriff well enough that time. She exhaled a wheezing sound followed by a low moan as she shrank back into the house.

Clint stood ramrod straight and shifted his gaze from the Sheriff to Jake and out to Caulfield at the truck. "You'd best all come in. Seems we have some talking to do." Despite his stoic tone, all the years came crushing down on the old man as he hobbled back through the door and to his wife who'd settled at the kitchen table.

The home was actually rather cold and not just because of the bad news. Both the Kincaids wore sweaters and a meager fire crackled in a pot belly stove just off the kitchen. Otherwise the home was decorated circa 1980s like the outside of the one-story structure. Clint placed a wrap over his wife's shoulder and hugged her as sobs wracked her torso.

Jake followed the Sheriff in, both men removing their hats. "Clint ... Margret, I am very sorry about Stephen," he said.

Both heads nodded, Clint successfully holding back tears. Margret continued to sob and wring her hands in the knee-length apron. Jake blinked and sniffed twice, keeping tears from welling up, pressure building deep between his eyes. This was a parent's worst nightmare.

"We don't think it was an accident," the Sheriff said. "He was shot at the trailhead leading to Horse Thief Ridge ... Jake's the one who found him."

More sobbing.

Clint glanced from Jake to the Sheriff and then toward a back bedroom. The Sheriff picked up on the action. "Are you all home alone, Clint?"

Kincaid pulled out a chair and sat down. "Yeah, Mathew is off to Sioux City trying to arrange some feed lot contracts. Shirley's married and lives in Omaha." Mathew, a couple years younger than Jake, had been a talented wide-receiver. Jake breathed deeply, trying to catch his breath—remembering kinder, simpler days.

Between sobs Margret mumbled, "He just got home. It's Christmas."

Clint took her hands in his and interlaced the fingers.

"Folks, I am deeply sorry to bring you this news," the Sheriff began. "Stephen is at the medical center in Palmer. The coroner will have to keep him a few days due to the nature of his death. Sorry again."

"Right," Clint sighed. "I've got some coffee on if either of you'd like some"

"That would be great, Clint," the Sheriff said. "There are a few questions I need to ask, I'm afraid. Unfortunately time is working against us with this storm comin' in and all."

Jake accepted a coffee also, and like the Sheriff, sipped it black and was grateful. Clint offered them chairs, and once seated, the Sheriff wasted no time. Notepad in hand he dove in. "Do either of you know anyone who might want to hurt Stephen ... someone with a grudge or who may have made threats against him?"

Margret shook her head and Clint said, "No, at least not here in Palmer." Clint blinked his eyes and stared at the table for a moment. "You know, Stephen's been up in Canada for the last nine months. He just got home last Wednesday."

"What was he doing up there?" the Sheriff asked. He'd written nothing so far in his notepad.

Jake held the coffee in two hands and enjoyed the warmth. The Kincaid home was typical of most ranch homes. The entire paneled wall to the right of the front door was covered with graduation pictures, a wedding party and several group photographs—a few in black and white.

The Sheriff continued his interview honing in on Stephen's activities and probing for any problems or trouble he might have been in. Jake noticed Clint Kincaid repeatedly glancing at the first bedroom off the family room. As it turned out, when asked by the Sheriff, he identified it as Stephen's room.

A quick survey of the room by the Sheriff revealed a rather sophisticated computer, a cloth-back rolling suitcase, several pairs of shoes, and clothes—mostly still in the suitcase. Jake noticed the lack of pictures in the room but a copy of the Koran sitting on the bedside stand. Clint caught Jake's eye as he focused on the leather-bound book. Jake wanted to ask if Stephen had converted to Islam but kept his mouth shut like he'd been instructed.

"I apologize for the inconvenience." The Sheriff waved his hand across the room. "But I need to close up the room and have my crime scene guys go over it with a fine-toothed comb ... See if we can start making some sense out of all this."

He called Caulfield into the house and posted him at the kitchen table with instructions that no one enter the room again until the crime scene crew had done their work. "And make sure they bring the computer in."

The deputy set a cup of coffee that Clint Kincaid had poured him on a sofa table and moved the chair directly in front of the bedroom door. It was apparent that Sheriff Schafer expected his orders to be followed explicitly.

Margret had stopped sobbing and now sat sniffling on the sofa, a handkerchief pressed to her nose. Clint put a hand on her shoulder and glanced at Jake, but would not hold eye contact.

"Clint, Margret," the Sheriff said. "I am very sorry for your loss. I assure you we will do everything in our power to get answers as to why this happened." He shifted his hat about in his hand, and shook his head. "Please call if anything else comes to mind. Even the smallest detail could be very important."

Jake followed the Sheriff through the door and they both put their hats back on as Clint closed the front door and turned off the porch light.

Back in the truck the Sheriff radioed in for a crime scene crew from Rapid City to load up and head out to the Kincaid ranch. He stroked his mustache and stared back at the house silhouetted in the darkening landscape.

To the east a coyote howled. The heaviness in Jake's heart eased some at the uplifting sight of the blinking Christmas lights. Atop the house a lighted cross suddenly went dark.

"I'm sure you noticed the Koran on the bedside stand." Jake broke his self-imposed silence.

"Yeah." The Sheriff pumped the gas and revved the engine. "I think Clint is not telling us everything either." He rolled down the window and spit a chew of tobacco. "I'll give him till tomorrow to come clean with me."

"He's got a lot to think about tonight." The law enforcement officer in Jake tried to sync with the Sheriff. "A dead son and all." Jake bent and straightened his bad knee several times.

The Sheriff set his hat on the seat between them and tipped his chin up slightly.

"You think Stephen was into something?" Jake asked the sixty-four-dollar question.

"Time will tell." The Sheriff glanced back toward Horse Thief Ridge. "Lots of pieces to this puzzle I think." He rolled the window up and eased the truck toward Boxelder Road. "We've got our work cut out for us ... three crime scenes already ... potentially."

"You better be quick, Sheriff," Jake said. "I think we'll all be snowed in by the middle of the week."

"First priority is to search that ridgeline from where the kid was probably shot."

Jake shook his head. "Like I said, I know where the trailhead is, but I think I may have been up there once in the past five years."

The Sheriff drummed on the leather-covered steering wheel. "I think I know someone who has been all over that and the next couple of ridgelines." The rear of the truck slid on ice as he turned onto the main road into Palmer. "Hopefully they've got your truck pulled out of the emergency room doors." He chuckled.

Jake's heart pounded up into his temples, forcefully ... not painful. Back to the emergency room, back to Tracy Aspen. The trusting, innocent Dakota cowgirl who at one time had been willing to give him the world. Wonder what she thought of the world now days? Wonder what she thought of him?

Chapter 4

Patriot's Hospital, Palmer

"We can close 'em but the automatic door, she will not work." Manuel Desoto, the hospital maintenance supervisor, placed the crowbar he'd used to reset the emergency doors into a large drawer at the bottom of his work cart. He squinted up at Tracy as he wiped his hands with a rag from the back pocket of his overalls.

At five foot eight, Tracy towered over the stocky middle-aged Hispanic, who couldn't be much over five foot.

"I get the contractors out from Rapid City by morning. It will not be a problem. A new track, I think." He smiled, showing shiny metal fillings that distracted one's attention from the scattering of pock marks on his dark-toned face.

"Can we manually open the door in case of another emergency?" Tracy asked. "We may need to get a patient through that entrance if an ambulance comes in or if we have a transfer."

"Oh sure, no problem. The track might get stuck open though. You call me. I be right back and get it closed up again."

Patriot's Hospital operated like many small community hospitals. During the daytime, no doctor stood duty in the emergency room, though Dr. Billingsly's office was just across the parking lot in the Medical Plaza if need be. Usually the staff just sent patients to his office or to a specialist if that was what Tracy, the triage nurse, decided. That was what she'd been hired for eight weeks earlier, fresh off active duty.

The sudden appearance of Jake Moran had caught her off guard. Clearly, she'd had a school girl crush on the older football player. She really hadn't felt the flutter and flush like she had today ... since high school.

He'd had it rough since graduating. Ten years that had definitely tested his faith. Tracy sighed deeply, probably reading way too much into things. After all, with a shooting and the boy dying, there were a lot of emotions flying around. Not to mention the amount of coffee she'd consumed.

Nonetheless, Palmer still felt like home and she would not miss Helmand Province or Kandahar. When she'd left nursing school, the draw of military service and solving the problems of the world seemed a noble goal. She'd always sought to live by the Christian precepts of faith, hope, and love. Her love for the Afghan people though, especially the tribal and religious leaders, had been sorely tested the last six months. As a consequence, faith and hope had likewise suffered.

She, along with Sam Whitcomb and Alexis, the receptionist and overall gopher for the emergency room, made short work of cleaning the trauma bay. With the unfortunate boy's body tucked away in the morgue, the next agenda item fell to ordering a late lunch. Hospital food, though tolerable, did not ignite any culinary cravings.

Her thoughts drifted once again to Jake Moran, a struggling rancher now. Her father had confessed that he didn't know the whole story behind Jake's firing from the National Park Service. And what was with the Sheriff's reference to the militia? Was that the old Wyoming Militia that had ruined her aunt's family and so enraged her own mother? Tracy had heard nothing about the armed outcasts since returning to South Dakota. Was there a South Dakota Militia?

Catapulting over the hood of his truck, Jake had appeared thinner than she remembered from high school. She almost didn't recognize him. Sometimes that meant depression, eating and sleeping disturbances.

He didn't appear gaunt by any means. His arms where muscular and well cut when he'd been doing CPR. She couldn't imagine him with the militia.

Like an apparition, he was standing in front of her again. *Why?*

"What ... what are you doing here?" She gulped.

A half-smile creased the side of his right cheek, accentuated by a crooked eyebrow. The face was a little weathered and deeply tanned, but the smile was the one that had always made her knees shake. She sat down behind the reception desk.

Muscles strained under his denim shirt as he leaned an arm on the counter. "I need to pick up my truck." His pale blue eyes studied her. "The Sheriff is parking ... said he had a few more questions."

"Questions for me?" *What now?* "Did you find anything out at your ranch?"

"Nothing much at the trailhead—some blood—that was about it. Sounded like he wanted to talk to both of us though." He held her gaze.

Tempted, she suspected, to check out her breasts like most men. Somehow he managed restraint and eased his attention instead to the metal C-clamp holding the electronic ambulance door in place.

He'd always been well-mannered. Back in high school he'd stop on cold mornings to offer her rides in his fairly new truck. She wasn't sure if it was manners or fear that held him back in the hay loft with her, the skinny adolescent. Now at age twenty-eight with an athletic frame and a few more pounds, she at least had respectable curves. She'd even competed in military biathlons—though deployments to Iran and Afghanistan had cut that short.

"I'm sorry about earlier," he said. "I never expected to run into you when I crashed into the emergency doors."

"Lots of changes since high school." Tracy pushed a wayward strand of hair behind her ear. "And, I've been away quite a while—college and all."

"Right," he said. The sparkle of his eyes faded as he blankly stared at the unlit Christmas tree across the waiting room.

"You're ranching now?"

"Trying to ... I'm making ends meet." He smiled weakly.

More than trying, he was actually doing pretty well according to her father. "Your mom must be proud of you, with getting the ranch up and going and all."

"Better now, yeah." He diverted his gaze out the windows. "It was hard for a while with the Park Service thing."

She could imagine the months of investigations and depositions. It had to have been demoralizing. She knew he hadn't reached out to the church for help. She'd never seen him at any of the services after his dad's funeral and certainly not since her return to Palmer. His mom and sister had shown up at Christmas or Easter sometimes—not Jake.

A hollowness gripped her chest as she recalled the great part her faith had had in her ability to accept the death and devastation of war. She recognized a few post-traumatic stress issues since returning but nothing like what she'd seen in the frontline Marines and Special Forces. How could anyone endure such tragedies of life without faith?

Reflexively, she reached up and placed her hand over his. She'd done this a thousand times with patients, in school, and on the battlefield. His muscles tensed, yet he did not pull away. It was the healing touch her Lakota grandmother had spoken of. And, although only one-quarter Lakota, Tracy had it—she'd had it as long as she could remember. While not the miraculous touch of Jesus, it had never failed at easing pain and suffering.

A long strand of dark hair fell across her face as she held Jake's gaze. Neither of them breathed.

"Great, I've got both of you here." Sheriff Schaffer pushed through the working single emergency room door. "We ain't had a murder in Palmer in over five years. And this storm is gonna really mess things up. I need some help."

Jake pulled his hand away slowly and reluctantly broke the stare. "You can't be serious. What am I going to do at this point?"

He unzipped his coat and slid his hat onto the counter. Long oily strands of hair, salt and pepper like his mustache, coursed down across his furrowed brow. "Miss Aspen." He nodded cordially. "Have you gotten any results back on the young Kincaid's toxicology or blood tests?"

"Blood work should be back, but the toxicology can take a week or more. That all gets sent out ... only the blood electrolytes and counts are done in-house."

"Okay, we'll just have to wait on the toxicology. Blood work should be done though, right?"

"It should all be in his chart or the computer, whenever you want it," Tracy said.

The Sheriff, tight-lipped with an eyebrow raised, looked at Jake and then back to Tracy. A slight smile cracked the side of his mouth. "Can you get off early today?" he asked her.

"Yeah, I guess. Phyllis is coming in ... should be here any minute now. Why?"

"I called your dad, but he's all the way out by Lead ... won't be back in town till Christmas Eve."

What did that have to do with anything? She glanced at Jake who frowned. The subtle flush under his tanned skin fading into the weathered wrinkle lines.

"Rail maintenance," she said. "They've been up that way every-day for the past two weeks." Her father was a lifer with the Burlington Northern Santa Fe line.

The Sheriff exhaled deeply. "I need to be up on the rim above Boxelder Gulch as soon as the weather clears or we're gonna miss any chance at examining the crime scene."

"Dad's hunting lease," she said, nodding.

Jake's eyes widened as he glanced between Tracy and the Sheriff. "Up above my ranch?"

"I guess," she said. "He and his railroad buddies have had that lease for nearly thirty years."

"Who owns the property?" the Sheriff asked.

"Some Trust out of Denver, the last I was aware. That was years ago."

"You know the trails and shooting lanes up on the rim?" The Sheriff studied Tracy, not blinking.

Now she knew where this was going. "Like the back of my hand. Got my first elk from that very ridge."

"That's what your pa said." He studied Jake. "I've got to stop over at the department and pick up a couple of technicians and their equipment ... Can you two get together climbing gear and meet me at the trail head to Horse Thief Ridge?"

"What?" Jake stepped back. "There's a hell of a snow storm clos-ing in on my ranch and I haven't got a damn thing done all day. Why do you need me?"

"Actually, son, I need your truck more than you." The Sheriff slapped Jake on the back with his hat as he tuned to leave. Dust drifted to the polished hospital floor. "But you've got nearly ten years in law enforcement. Bring your rifle and I'll bring a deputy's badge."

Tracy slid between the two testy men. "You obviously haven't seen the weather scan," she said to the Sheriff.

"Hell, don't tell me ... Geez." The Sheriff gazed out the frosted-over window. "The State boys in Rapid City are gonna have my ass for a killin' with no evidence."

"Suppose to be a lull for twelve hours or so in the morning." Tracy stood back from the Sheriff who smelled like he'd taken his long-johns out of a cedar chest full of mothballs. A whiff of pine from the Yankee candle burning on the reception desk worked to rekindle her Christmas spirit.

"The morning then." The Sheriff poked his finger on Jake's chest.

The ex-ranger did not budge.

Tracy exhaled. A tightness in her chest eased. The Sheriff must not have harbored any fears of Jake's involvement with the militia, if he was deputizing the former ranger.

Fellow nurse Phyllis Middleton, wearing sunglasses, ambled by and threw a half-wave at Tracy. "Sorry, Boss ... The Packers play like Girl Scouts. I think it's all fixed to tell ya the truth."

"Well, you missed all the action here." Tracy tossed a ring full of keys on the counter. "You're in charge. Apparently we're being deputized."

Chapter 5

Palmer, South Dakota

It would be dark before Jake could get back to the ranch. Large flakes created a shimmering veil across his headlights as dusk settled over Palmer. The church sat silently up a rise to the west, Pastor Paul futilely shoveling the sidewalk from the stained oak doors to the road. A single flood light illuminated the ageless nativity scene now only three-quarters visible under a heavy layer of snow.

He swallowed hard at the realization that there would likely be a Christmas funeral, just before or after the holiday. The pressure behind his eyes returned. He sniffed unconsciously as he turned toward downtown. The back of the truck slid to the left and he gently eased the steering wheel in the same direction to correct—probably time to put some sand in the bed for better traction.

He idled the old pickup down the ice-covered Main Street as the decorative candlesticks, Christmas trees, and candy canes on the light posts glowed with holiday cheer. *We Three Kings* echoed from the brightly lit windows of the Mountain Rose Café. The aroma of hot apple cider and cinnamon pulled the lump out of his throat and warmed his chest as he pushed through the front door.

"Look at what the cat drug in." His mother chuckled from the service window of the kitchen. She blew her bangs away from her eyes and pushed them back up into a hair net. Just shy of fifty, her bright eyes and sharp facial lines still testified to her youthful Scandinavian beauty.

His kid sister, Catherine, efficiently placed a mountainous order of food in front of an eager family of six—smiled and waved her left hand, complete with white gold engagement ring. The chalkboard next to the modern mini-computer cash register read, *Chicken Parmesan with Linguine.*

"What's the special?" Jake hollered to his mother over the first bars of *Silent Night.* He never missed a chance to poke fun at her if the special didn't include beef.

"For you, cowboy, it's hamburger steak with chicken gravy." She rang the bell on the heated service bar and pointed teasingly at him.

Jake eyed the crowded counter, snatched a menu from behind the register, and maneuvered to a small table in the back. Two computer nerds sat off to the right pecking away at wireless keyboards.

Catherine's Christmas earrings literally lighted up as she swept into the chair across from him. He sat facing the front door—a habit he'd developed since being shot at from the back a few years earlier. Rudolph's red nose and Santa's ruby cheeks flashing on Catherine's ears contrasted with the miniature nativity perched on the elevated shelf across the back of the Mountain Rose.

"A white Christmas," Catherine bubbled excitedly, then frowned. "You get the cattle in okay?"

"All buttoned up in a barn full of hay," Jake said. "They're a little antsy still but they'll settle in fine."

"You stayin' in town tonight?" Catherine asked as she glanced through the front window at fluffy snow flakes magnified in the street lights. "Most of the weather computer models have us getting over twenty and maybe as much as thirty-three inches of snow."

"You'd be the one to know." Jake nodded toward the new mini-computer.

"Mom finally let me upgrade that aging Gateway." She crossed her legs and leaned in close, giving Jake a kiss on the cheek.

She smelled of wild sage and Jake immediately felt his taut shoulders relax. He hadn't realized how uptight the day had gotten him. He tipped his head. "Stephen Kincaid is dead."

Catherine sat upright. "How? Just now ... today I mean?"

"Out north of the ranch ... the trailhead up to Horse Thief Ridge." Jake placed his hand on Catherine's. "He was shot."

She pulled her hand loose and put both over her mouth as she inhaled sharply.

The pressure again settled behind Jake's eyes. He blinked slowly and took her hands. "The Sheriff is investigating ... The circumstances are ... unclear."

"You've been out with the Sheriff?" Her eyes narrowed.

"We stopped at the Kincaids and told his parents."

Her head shook as she exhaled slowly through her nose.

The climbing death of fellow park ranger Bret Peterson two years back had also started with the Sheriff investigating. What happened in the weeks that followed mimicked the Salem witch trials. States Attorneys and FBI investigators—it had been a mess. In the end, Sheriff Schaffer told Jake he was lucky not to have been indicted.

A fast-talking Sioux City lawyer aided by the quick and penetrating computer interrogations of Catherine had redirected the probe elsewhere—though Jake had not been left unscathed.

"They are not your friends, Jake," she said.

Jake sat back. "The Sheriff is okay ... It's those Federal jackasses who are just out to get notches on their guns."

"Watch your back," she said. "Do you want me to keep an eye on what they're doing?"

He knew she could do that. A computer science degree in Business and Internet Marketing developed a definite skill set. He'd seen the results that his attorney showed him only under the guise of attorney-client privilege—not all totally legal he suspected. But for her big brother, Catherine would pull out all the stops.

"Whoa! Not yet, Cat." He'd called her that since she'd started to crawl. "But I'll let you know ... I don't trust these guys any farther than I can throw 'em."

"So ... stayin' the night or not."

"If you guys aren't filled up with sleep-overs."

She slugged his shoulder. "Stewart is on a run over to Billings. They're getting ready for the storm."

Stewart, her fiancé, managed feed lots for Hormel across the Midwest. His expertise, as best Jake could determine, involved something to do with maximization of mitochondrial protein synthesis. Whatever it was, his tips for Jake's herd had definitely paid off.

"He didn't leave his feed lot boots in your breezeway again, did he?" Jake pinched his nostrils.

"That never really happened you know." Catherine blushed. "He left them on the porch. Just so happened it was a hot ninety-plus day with no wind." She stuck a pencil in her hair. "Mom's got the guest room all cleaned up. She was figuring you'd need it some with the Nor-wester blowin' in." She stood and pushed the chair in.

"I need to head back out early, but I'd much rather drive in the daylight than at night," he said.

"You want the special ... the one on the board, not the one you and Mom fight over?"

"String beans, if you've got some hot, and a cup of decaf." He smiled and handed over the menu. "Stewart still helping out some in the back?"

"He likes cooking ... does tend to have your hankering for beef though." She waved at a group near the front window. "Mom will have to adjust. It's not like this is chicken territory."

Jake laughed while his mother "evil eyed" him from the kitchen. It was clear his plans of celebrating Christmas at the ranch with the two was not going to happen. It was to be the beginning of a healing year for him—with his family's help. Somehow he'd manage to be with them. If he came to town though he'd probably have to attend church. That would take some mental preparation.

Catherine winked as she maneuvered to the front table with a tray of cinnamon spiced hot apple cider.

•

Tracy picked her way across the icy asphalt onto the salted sidewalk. The crunching of her Dansko nursing shoes accentuated the chilly freshness of the nighttime mountain air. Biting wind whipped the scarf around her neck with each calculated step up the slippery ramp from the ambulance entrance. Fine particles of snow dashed across her feet like a handful of flour thrown into a stiff breeze, but the flakes falling from the sky now were fat and plump.

Her cheeks stung from the unrelenting onslaught. Mercifully, South Dakota wasn't as cold as the Hindu Kush Mountains had been last Christmas ... and there was no cracking of automatic-weapons fire or bomb concussions. Despite the howling wind, she could still detect the welcoming fragrance of Ponderosa Pine.

Luckily her standard road tires from California still managed a reasonable grip on the road as she coaxed her Ford Focus around sweeping curves to her apartment. She could probably get back up to the hospital in the morning but getting back after a snow storm might be a push. If she left her car in the hospital parking lot it might be there all winter.

She probably needed snow tires or chains. She'd never done that herself. Her dad had always taken care of that in high school and her brothers, Matt and Kevin, had told her to stop procrastinating but neither had offered to help. The metal and ice crackled when she turned the key in the door of the cherry red compact.

She was stripped naked within a minute, jumped into a quick shower and then to her flannel pajamas before the Dakota cold had a chance to invade her body. After dumping her scrubs in the washing machine, she surveyed her culinary options, basically frozen dinners. Everything else came in a can. She eyed the Betty Crocker cookbook her mother had given her as a homecoming present—you probably needed ingredients to make a home-cooked meal.

Or! Two blocks through the snow and she'd be at the Mountain Rose.

◆

Jake glanced up from his coffee and did a double-take. Tracy was standing at the front counter helping his mother with the computer. He swallowed hard as the tension returned to his neck. Tracy moved the wireless mouse and punched a few sites on the tool bar. His mother nodded and placed her hand comfortably on Tracy's shoulder—then resumed typing on the keyboard.

Catherine slipped an order on the service window wheel. "She just starts pushing buttons when she gets confused," she said to Tracy. "Sometimes she ends up in the weirdest places."

There seemed a familiarity between the two women.

Tracy removed a knitted stocking cap, scarf and western print wool jacket. Underneath, the cardigan sweater and designer jeans complimented her shapely figure. Jake fought the flush he knew was climbing into his face. For what reason he wasn't sure, but he found himself rising from his chair.

Tracy smiled brightly first at Catherine and then at him. "Thought I might find you here," she said. Catherine laid a menu on the table across from Jake. Tracy raised an eyebrow.

His sister nodded to the chair across from Jake. "Have a seat … it's a little crowded in here tonight." She made a sisterly face at Jake. "You two do know each other … right?"

His face felt like a cast iron stove. "Yeah, of course." He awkwardly shifted around the table and held the chair out for Tracy.

She grinned through tight lips, dimples showing. "You sure?"

"Absolutely … though I have to say I feel a little set up."

Catherine laughed. "You guys started it—not me."

Tracy's stare had turned stern.

Catherine did not back down. "Come on," she said to Tracy. "Lighten up."

Jake squirmed in his seat. "Am I missing something here?"

"Science Club," Tracy said.

"Science Club?" Jake studied the two women.

Catherine glanced about the restaurant. "Yeah, Science Club." She leaned near Jake with her hand on the table. "Your computer nerd sister and biology nerd, almost girlfriend … were in the high school Science Club for three years."

The "almost girlfriend" comment told him that the two had been more than just fellow club members. He rubbed his hand through his hair and across his neck. Thankfully the roasting sensation in his face seemed to be easing.

Catherine stood upright hands on hips as if challenging him.

"So … what does an ex-biology nerd have for dinner?" He asked Tracy as he noted the flaming face disease appeared to have jumped across the table to her.

Catherine answered for her. "How's the special sound?"

"Great, you've never done me wrong." Tracy smirked. "Seems I'm becoming a Mountain Rose regular."

Jake nodded.

Catherine pirouetted in her long serving dress and joined their mother at the front counter.

"How're you doing this evening?" Tracy asked.

"You mean with the shooting and all?"

"Yeah … you all talked with the Kincaids? That must have been tough." She stood and placed her coat over the back of the chair.

Jake watched her and said nothing. She sat back down and waited for him to speak.

"I don't know. Who would want to kill Stephen, and why?" He rubbed a thumb across the back of his hand and leaned closer to Tracy. "I have to tell you, there are some things happening around here the past few years I don't understand."

"In Palmer?"

"No. More up on the plateaus and in some of the dry gulches ... remote areas." He glanced to see if anyone was listening. "Maybe I'm just paranoid. I've pretty much tried to just concentrate on the ranch these past couple of years."

"Have there been other shootings ... murders?"

"Nothing near Palmer," Jake said. "They probably aren't even related."

Catherine breezed up with hot apple cider and tableware for Tracy. "Why such serious faces?" She frowned. "You guys should try and put the day behind you and enjoy dinner ... if you don't, Mom's gonna be real pissed."

Over her shoulder Jake could see his mother sneaking a glance their way between services. "Thanks, Cat. You try and keep Mom at bay ... okay?"

With a sly smirk and raised eyebrow she was on to the next table.

"Still a firecracker," Tracy said.

"Apparently a bit of a matchmaker also." Jake smoothed the napkin across his legs.

"She's got a memory like an elephant." Tracy leaned in. "I may have confided some of my schoolgirl fantasies back in the day."

"I had no idea ... honestly." Where to go from here? He felt the urge to squirm in his chair.

"No, no ... chill, Cowboy." Tracy buttered a roll. "Look, you were gone—off to college most of those years." She held his gaze. "Funny how things from a decade ago can kick up old emotions and memories."

Jake studied her over his coffee. Maybe, just maybe there was still a romantic fire in Tracy Aspen. Pressure pushed out against his chest, a fullness—actually a feeling of holiday hopefulness.

Dinner as always was hot and delicious. They talked of school mates and Tracy was excited to hear of a best friend, with whom she lost touch, being married and living just over in Hill City. She smiled at many of his stories but when he asked about Afghanistan she grew distant and he did not press the issue. And she didn't ask about his dismissal from the National Park Service.

She agreed to let him pick her up at her apartment in the morning.

Chapter 6

Palmer, South Dakota

A woman had never licked or kissed Jake's hand. Mesmerizing dark eyes drew him in. Luscious pink lips whispered sweet words he could not quite discern. He was pleasantly floating while nestled against soft womanly skin, Tracy's skin.

"Duke." Echoed through the bedroom door. "Duke, leave Jake alone. Come here boy." His mother's melodic voice replaced the enchanting woman of his dream. Duke continued to lather Jake's hand with drool. It would have been his neck and face if Duke could've reached him without jumping on the bed.

It was not Tracy, though the loving canine intent was obvious. Jake patted Duke's bristly head and scratched him gruffly behind the ears. Tail thumping like a drum, the ball of hair rocketed toward the kitchen at the rustle of a dog food bag. Duke, actually Duke II, was named after Jake's childhood dog, who in turn had been named "The Duke" after John Wayne.

Try as he could, he was unable to prevent the particulars of his dream from reluctantly melting away. The red bars on the digital clock formed six-twenty. It was not yet light but a hint of dawn touched the lace curtains.

"You got time for some breakfast?" his mother asked as he stumbled from the bed. The first mercy cup of coffee already sat steaming on a paper napkin over a doily on the bedside stand.

He sipped the coffee and calculated times in his head. "How about an egg sandwich ... Can you make that two?" he asked as he tip-toed into the bathroom on the cold linoleum.

"Do you think she would like cheese on hers?" His mother cooed. "That's a sweet girl ... I hope you know."

Jake turned on the shower without answering.

After toweling off, he slipped into a combination of old clothes he'd left at the house and one of his father's shirts. Catherine, with her cell phone on speaker, sat surfing the computer while talking to someone in Canada.

On the kitchen table sat two toasted egg sandwiches, sliced cheese on the side and a thermos of coffee—also his dad's. He kissed his mother on the cheek and whispered. "Tell Cat I'll let her know how things are going ... and yeah, I think Tracy is sweet, too."

A break in the cloud cover to the east projected an orange-copper hue onto the high cirrus cloud line to the west. The wind had died down but the snow accumulation had reached nearly a foot overnight. Jake shifted down to four-wheel drive and punched in Tracy's cell phone number as he approached her apartment complex. She answered on the third ring.

"Jake, you about ready?"

He told her about the egg sandwiches and coffee.

"I'll be down in five ... just got to powder my nose." She chuckled.

Jake watched Tracy clamor down from her second floor apartment. A little taller and more curvaceous than she'd been as a sophomore in high school. Green military fatigues under an orange hunting jacket and stocking cap covered all the feminine attributes she'd exhibited the night before.

Jake jumped out to help her just as she slammed a duffle bag and sturdy rifle case into the bed of his truck. She was not the scrawny girl he'd rescued from the wintery cold on the way to school years earlier. The athletic outline of her buttocks tugged at him as she slid her hips up into the truck. Her imposing high Indian cheekbones defined a beauty that had matured remarkably. There were not many single women like her around the Black Hills.

She was fiery. He'd once heard her great-great or great-great-great grandfather had fought against Custer. Nothing people bragged about much these days in South Dakota. But he'd experienced a tenacious quality in Tracy even when she was a teenager.

♦

Tracy recognized the blanket covering the torn upholstery in the old Ford pickup. High school quarterback Jake Moran had been into football and trucks. He decidedly had not been enamored with cross-cultural issues and Dakota heritage. She rubbed her hand along the coarse wool fabric. Sweet memories of a patient grandmother and hot fires of cedar and spruce enveloped her.

"A gift from Gene Bearclaw." Jake threw his hat on the seat and glanced down at her hand dancing across the intricate stitching.

"Really?" Tracy watched as broad snowflakes blanketed the asphalt. Things did change over ten years, including the eagle feather hanging from the mirror by a braided leather strap. She nodded toward the feather. "That'll get you a big fine—even if you just found it lying next to the road."

"Not if I've got an Indian riding with me who'll claim it's hers." His sand-colored eyebrows raised in challenge.

"I wouldn't hold your breath for that one, Cowboy."

"Actually, it was also a gift from Bearclaw," Jake said.

Tracy gently stroked the wispy feather. Resolve and reassurance raced into her chest. She sighed deeply. Feathers were not given away casually.

Jake eased the old work truck out of the parking lot and directly into the swirling, drifting snow. Leafless oaks and aspens swayed like empty sentinels against the Canadian storm.

"Sam Whitcomb says we're in for a big blow for Christmas," she said. The weather had always seemed a safe topic with men.

"That ol' Indian should know. He's seen enough winters in the Black Hills."

Tracy punched weather on her iPhone, held it up to Jake as they stopped at one of three stoplights in Palmer. "Crap, they're predicting eighteen to thirty inches across the south of the state."

"Cat said she thought it could get to nearly three feet," Jake said.

He down-shifted and readjusted the heater. His sandy blond hair jumped about with each bounce of the old truck. Repeatedly, he ran his fingers through the unruly mane, tucking it behind his ears.

Tracy licked her lips as she imagined her hands in those golden curls. The same thoughts she'd had ten years earlier.

He glanced at her and broke into a beautiful white-toothed smile. "So what brought you back to Palmer?"

Where was this going? Certainly not him. Was that what he was thinking? Heat flared in her cheeks. She turned so he wouldn't notice. On Main Street, scattered business lights announce the grudging dawn of a new day. "It was the best job offer, best experience." That was enough. He didn't need to know any more.

"Probably nice to be out of the military. That regimentation stuff gets old."

"Kinda like the Park Service." She regretted saying it instantly. Pressure in her chest pushed a choking sensation into her throat.

Jake stopped behind a snowplow, forearm muscles flexing on the steering wheel and mouth held tight. "I guess."

"And now you're a rancher," Tracy said, breaking the silence. "Just like when you were growing up."

"Just like when I was growing up," he said, nodding. He took a deep breath and rubbed his callused hand along the woven blanket on the seat. "Some things have changed a lot since high school." His left eyebrow rose with a lady-killer smirk.

"What, I'm not the nerd reservation girl that you gave rides to anymore?"

"You were never a reservation girl. Your dad worked for the railroad." He scoffed.

"Well, I did spend some time on the reservation with my grandmother."

"Ceremonies and things." He shifted back into gear as the snow plow turned up a side street. "She lived in Rapid City ... didn't she?"

Tracy did the grown-up thing, turned toward him and stuck her tongue out. "Smarty pants," she said.

"That's the Tracy Aspen I remember," he chuckled, then turned serious. "She still alive ... your grandmother?"

Tracy's stomach turned over and twisted. "She passed when I was deployed. It was real hard on my mom for awhile ... especially seems to be hard around harvest time, and Christmas of course." She tried to smile but her cheeks wouldn't cooperate.

Silently they turned toward the outskirts of Palmer.

He stared at her while they waited for the last stoplight out of town, and not with a religious Christmas-type adoration. He was a virile man who, as best she judged, had no wife or steady girlfriend. That meant he was probably in a state of sexual starvation. Something Tracy could not think of with a dead boy lying in the morgue, a dead boy with a peacock feather in his coat—a sign of sorts to the Lakota and a symbol of guardianship for Muslims.

There was more, too. Her mother was right about the idiot militia. They were every bit as whacky as the Islamic fundamentalists. Terrorists had no boundaries. And Jake definitely had a stick up his hind-end about the federal authorities. The question was how far up it went?

Through the flurries an occasional ray of sunshine blazed off the newly fallen snow. It certainly looked a lot more like Christmas than Kandahar had last year. The town had changed some—a few new stores and one more stop light. A murder. A sigh escaped her pressured chest. Still, she preferred home, family, and old friends to the world stage.

She pulled the laboratory printouts from the hospital out of her backpack. There'd been no time to get a urine specimen but the coroner would examine that. Tracy skimmed the results. A low normal hemoglobin, which is typical in a trauma, no time for the blood to equilibrate or react to the massive hemorrhage. The victim bleeds out while all the blood test look normal—the blood just isn't in the body anymore.

A vision of cold tents with blood-covered operating tables interposed itself over the pristine Yule Tide landscape of Palmer and then was gone. She shivered though the inside of the truck was still warm.

What is this? Stephen Kincaid's white blood cell count read five-hundred. It should have been ten times that level, thirty times after epinephrine had been given. But she'd drawn the blood when she first got the intravenous line in, the epinephrine came afterward. And geez! His platelet count sat at under twenty-thousand. Again, one tenth of what it should be. No wonder he bled out.

Could the sample have come from an intravenous line with saline running, diluted? No, she'd drawn it directly from the vein, and the hemoglobin level was appropriate. What was going on with Stephen Kincaid?

And his electrolytes were out of kilter, too—low sodium and high potassium—the bicarbonate was also elevated. He'd been profoundly dehydrated before he'd ever been shot.

She reiterated the lab results to Jake shaking her head and fighting the tightness in her throat.

"Sounds like all Stephen had was bad luck on top of bad luck," Jake said.

"This is more than bad luck ... this is just weird."

Tracy rested her knees against the front console of the truck and tapped on her lips.

She'd seen this mix of lab results in the past. Not in the military but in nursing school at the University of Arizona—in cancer patients.

Chapter 7

Moran Ranch, Black Hills

Tracy surveyed the ramshackle fence line leading to an equally decrepit gate. All the gaps appeared to have been repaired but with materials she would have expected to see in a junk yard, rather than attached to a fence keeping in a herd of cattle. The third post out resembled the rear axle of her family's old Dodge truck.

Jake chewed on his lip and squinted through windshield wipers that fought to keep ahead of the snow. He used his glove to swipe away condensation on the inside of the window, pushed his stained cowboy hat up on his forehead, and turned off the main road.

Tracy squirmed on the seat unintentionally, a reaction she'd first noticed years earlier as an adolescent sitting in Jake's truck and watching the star quarterback chew that inviting lip. She readjusted herself and checked the door panel to see if the truck had seat heaters. It didn't.

The light banter they'd exchanged on the way out to the ranch had been replaced by silence as they rolled up to the south gate, fresh snow crunching under the wheels. The engine throttled down and the wailing wind encircled them.

"I don't think I've ever been into Boxelder Gulch this way before," she said. "I thought I knew all the back roads."

"Not surprising," Jake said. "There really isn't a road into the gulch from the ranch. You need to cut across the west pasture trail, and that takes a four-wheel drive."

"Yeah, I think we came in from below Horse Thief Ridge just above the Kincaid Ranch, most of the time anyway."

"You hunted with your dad?"

"And with a couple of the railroad guys. Jim Newman's daughter, Heather, also hunted. Was she in your class?"

"A year behind, I think." Jake tipped his head slightly. He sighed before breaking into a half-smile.

"What?"

"Nothing ... just a flashback to those days."

"Right." She smiled back. "Pleasant memories?"

He shifted his gaze out the truck window and scrunched the corner of his mouth. "Well, memories." He tapped on the steering wheel as he eased up the rutted drive and stopped before the closed gate. A jackrabbit scurried away from behind a fence post held up largely by a mound of prairie moonwort. "Welcome to the Lazy T ... at least what's left of it after the Tanners sold most of the acreage to Clint Kincaid and the Stephensens."

"How much were you able to get?"

"This quarter and another eighty acres across the ravine to the east. Lars Stephensen is leasing me another four hundred acres over south of the ravine as well. We attempt to negotiate a sale price on and off ... someday maybe."

"Sounds like a lot of work for one guy!" Tracy shouted into the wind as Jake swung out of the truck cab to unhitch the gate. She jumped out behind him. "I'll re-hook it—just don't spin mud at me."

"Been a while since I did that." He passed the wire loop of the gate to her and kicked muddy snow off his boots before climbing in behind the steering wheel.

Back in the truck, the isolated homestead of the ranch lay nearly a half-mile up a dirt road that was covered with bull thistle, sage leaf, and deepening snow. The truck bounced from side to side as Jake tried to avoid the biggest ruts.

"Geez, you could use a bit of road plowing out here." Tracy held tight to the hand-grip above the passenger's window.

"In the spring maybe," Jake said. "Have to see how the finances are. That's not a high priority."

His leather gloves gripped the steering wheel tightly. Taut forearm muscles reminded Tracy of his gridiron days. He sported a three- or four-day growth of beard. A smooth-shaven man was nice when the face action got heavy, but for everyday appeal the rough-and-tumble GQ look did tend to get her hormones running. She shook her head. She'd imagined over the years what Jake was up to, yet had never pictured the two of them in this circumstance.

The flashback hit!

•

A flash lit up the trailer two vehicles in front of them and simultaneously the concussion thundered through the hummer. Dirt and silt covered them. Marines flew out every door then dove behind a mortar wall next to the gravel access-road. The charred shell of the Afghan aid clinic sat just behind the wall, across a dusty square littered with burned and rusted vehicles.

Tracy followed the marines firing at the roof of an apartment complex above the clinic. Flashes of gunfire erupted from an upper-floor window. She emptied her sidearm in the general direction, hands shaking and her heart pounding in her chest.

"Keep your head down, Lieutenant ... and stop shooting." Hernandez, her Gunny Sergeant, forcefully pushed Tracy's head down near her knees. "That 9 mm ain't gonna do nothing anyway."

Spasms pounded between her aching ears. She struggled to recover from the concussion of the rocket-propelled grenade that had halted their approach.

Scattered shots ricocheted off the protective wall. She was supposed to be relieving Lieutenant Commander Novak at the clinic today—so much for plans.

From fifty yards down the wall, Marines concentrated automatic weapons fire on the roof of the dilapidated housing unit.

The sergeant vaulted the stone wall like a gymnast. He sprinted behind a burned-out tanker truck to the north. No return fire. He threw himself through the clinic's partially open door. Shots echoed from the structure accompanied by flashes from the window.

Medical bag in hand, Tracy scrambled over the wall and crawled to the clinic door. Riflemen swept the housing complex up the hillside with blasts of their automatic weapons.

She gasped as fear squeezed her chest in a near death grip. Novak lay in a crimson pool, his right leg nearly severed, torso covered in blood, and half his jaw blown away. Hernandez bent over a young woman up against the far wall, battle pistol trained on a bullet-ridden Arab boy, pants down around his knees.

The girl's gray cotton abaya lay torn and pulled up around her chest—a bone-handled tribal knife jammed in her bloodied left shoulder. Naked from the waist down, she moaned, twisted, and withered away from the sergeant. Her uninjured hand thrust between her legs tried to cover bloody genitals. Tracy could just make out tape on either side of the girl's waist, wrapping around to her back.

Infrequent, dying heaves escaped from the lungs of the hemorrhaging, thinly bearded insurgent. His Kalashnikov rifle lay next to the girl.

Tears coursed down the girl's blood-stained cheeks. Barely a woman, she grimaced and sobbed. Gouges splayed across two of the interior walls testified to the voracity of the attack. Novak was dead. The boy would be soon, maybe the girl as well.

Hernandez tugged, one-handed, at the tape on the girl's side. "Watch her, Lieutenant." He glanced quickly around the room. "She's got something taped to her back … could be a bomb. Don't let her move."

Hernandez bent his head around the side of the girl, following the tape. He leaned back and pushed his Colt M45 battle pistol at Tracy. "Here," he said. "Shoot her if she goes for a wire or switch."

Tracy fumbled to holster her 9mm Beretta. Could she actually shoot the girl?

He carefully rolled the whimpering Afghan up onto her good shoulder. Still, she screamed, eyes burning in panic. Tracy's stomach lurched, a sour taste rising into the back of her mouth. Babbling in Pashtun, the eyes of the dark-haired girl begged Tracy—right hand continuing to cover her violated genitalia. Tracy understood little of the young woman's pleading. Hernandez ripped the tape and a thin pack of photocopies off her bloodied back

She snarled and under her breath mumbled in English, "Let me die."

Hernandez grabbed back the .45 and uprighted a broken table. "No wires … She's clear." He kicked the insurgent's rifle away from the girl and placed the papers on the table.

"I can't remove this knife until she's in an operating room where the bleeding can be controlled." Tracy knelt over the girl who, with closed eyes, lay silently taking short labored breaths. "Right now the bleeding is minimal, but she's lost a lot of blood … could still bleed to death."

A slim corporal poked his head in the door. "We're clear." He stepped next to Hernandez. "Russian?" he asked, peering over the sergeant's shoulder at the papers spread on the broken table.

Hernandez turned abruptly. "Yeah, and I don't think she was with these other guys either." He flipped through pages and then rubbed a hand across the back of his neck.

Tracy placed the gauze pads from Novak's trauma bag onto the girls shoulder and turned to find the sergeant studying the girl. On the table lay a Russian document with various cylinders and circles diagramed. At the top, the bold Cyrillic letters were followed by the number *115*.

"If you can save her, she's gonna need to be interrogated." Hernandez folded the papers and slid them into the back pouch of his vest. He grabbed the corporal's arm. "Leave the boy. Get someone to help the lieutenant with the girl, and bag Novak." He stared blankly out to the dry dirt-covered compound. "You guys find any of the technicians?"

"One behind a water barrel out back." The corporal ejected a spent magazine from his M16 and inserted a new one. "He said the two Afghan techs ran off just when the attack started."

"Okay, we're out of here in five. Got it?"

"Roger, Sarg. Rolling in five."

•

Her pulse slammed up into her ears as she fought to control breathes that tore at her chest. Jake's old pickup rattled and squeaked with each bounce and jerk. Maybe this is what she needed to do. Confront these demons in the daytime so they would leave her alone at night. Incrementally, finally, air slipped smoothly into her lungs, without gasps and gulps. Pounding pressure eased from the base of her skull.

Jake concentrated on control of the beaten truck. He'd not noticed her near break. Perhaps she'd over-thought the whole episode. A leathery scent mixed with a near briny male muskiness inside the truck cab additionally helped ground her.

The dull, wood-sided farmhouse stood amongst a handful of leafless aspen with a windbreak of mature white or Black Hills spruce to the west. They approached from the south. In front and to the left, the terrain dropped off toward a ravine. To the right, a gentle rise created a shallow basin where the partly dismantled house and three outbuildings, in various levels of repair, all faced in toward the center.

Tracy swallowed hard and relaxed her grip on the door handle. "Tearing down or rebuilding?"

"A little of both." Jake eased the truck into an open-front shed.

The battered doors sat at acute angles against the far wall, rotted cross beams unable to support even the weight of the weathered boards. On further examination, she realized that without the rusted hinges they'd just be a pile of rotting lumber.

"I'll just be a minute." He turned toward a small corral behind a barn that sported a new coat of red paint. "Gotta turn out some feed for a couple of calves."

"Okay for me to use the little girl's room?" Tracy nodded toward the homestead.

"I guess … it isn't much yet." Jake took off his felt cowboy hat and brushed a hand through wind-blown hair before scrunching the hat firmly back down.

She slung her Fossil purse over her shoulder and slid down into ankle-deep snow. "As long as you have running water, it'll be better than a medevac tent. I do have to admit though—the Marines did try to make it a little easier on us women." She squinted against a flicker of sunlight and tried to resurrect a little smile.

He stared back, a slight furrow to his brow, nodded, and turned toward the barn. "Have at it then … it's not locked."

Was he thinking of her as the kid tomboy he'd teased incessantly? Had ten years changed his opinion of her at all? Jake rounded the corner of the barn. He still had the confident swaggering gait of an athlete, ease of movement like the flowing twitch of a white-tailed deer. Beyond the grove of trees a cooper's hawk circled, dancing erratically with the buffeting wind, searching for dinner.

A series of cut logs served as the three steps to the porch and a broken-down railing lay stacked at the far end beneath the large bay window. The porch smelled of fresh treated pine and felt solid. New yellow, green, and red wires poked out of ankle-level metal outlet boxes at either end of the porch. The modern comforts of home—eventually. The house had probably been a comfortable and warm respite against the South Dakota winters at one time.

A solid oak door swung in without a squeak and revealed a clean, but Spartan, living room. Hardwood floors showed the remnants of linoleum and carpet that had been stripped away. The large fireplace had bricking halfway up and the mantle stood leaning in the corner next to the bay windows. Actually, the floors were clean swept and no dirty dishes sat in the sink.

A plate and a Mount Rushmore coffee cup sat upside down drying on a towel. The silent ceiling fan lazily rotated. Surprisingly, an ornate golden oak sideboard and dinning table with chairs spruced the kitchen area nicely.

Musky masculinity pushed a fullness from her chest into her face obliging a half-smile. As she exhaled her heart skipped a beat. Enough snooping. The downstairs bathroom featured a claw-footed cast-iron tub, big enough for two in a pinch.

She doubted it was original with the house. And no signs of a women's influence—no makeup, hair pins, or extra toothbrush— appeared scattered about the counter or sink. As she finished she heard the clump of boots going up the stairs just off the foyer.

•

The faint scent of a spicy-sage perfume lingered at the bottom of the stairwell as Jake two-stepped it up to his room.

The keen womanly fragrance was not that of the gangly kid he'd given rides to before leaving for Rapid City and college. A woman war veteran. He didn't recall ever knowing a woman who'd fought overseas. In fact he hadn't had much dealings with any women for over a year.

"Could use a woman's touch!" came bellowing from the ground floor.

He pulled a second box of .270 rounds from underneath his bed, turned, and hollered back through the open bedroom door, "I think it had plenty of that in the 60s."

He grabbed his hiking boots from beside his highboy and slipped a forest green fleece off a hanger. At the top of the stairs he caught a magical glint of light sparking from Tracy's amber eyes as she stared up the staircase.

The teasing face brought a hollow feel to his stomach. The place really did lack a woman.

"There're curtains, rugs, and even aprons piled up in the tool shed out back. Some of it may even be salvageable." He eased down the steps under Tracy's scrutiny. Feebly, he smirked.

"You're lucky you live in dry South Dakota," she said. "Most anywhere else, the damp and humidity would ruin it all."

The casual throw of her hip and relaxed banter blended naturally with the rustic farm house.

"The Tanners leave all that stuff behind?"

"The Tanners moved into a new house in Rapid City ... Sounded like the missus was redecorating in a big way." He scratched at his ear and glanced back toward the kitchen. "Left me all the worn-out farm crap, I guess."

"Well, it's clean, at least." A smile creased the edge of her ruby-red mouth.

He stood close above her on the stairs—her mouth inches from his belly. "Hopefully, I'll get to the house some this winter." He brushed his hand across her shoulder and rested it on the stair rail. "I still have fence work and a hayloft to get shipshape before the weather really sets in, as you squids would say."

"Careful, squid is not a term of endearment." Tracy took the hiking boots from his hand and started undoing the laces. She glanced down from his gaze and softened her voice. "Whatever happened to Natalie?"

Heat rose up his neck and a tightness pulled at the base of his skull. He'd never really addressed that issue. He'd simply walked away and never looked back, until now. He set the rifle shells on the foyer table as she redoubled her efforts at loosening the laces.

She didn't look up.

"Yeah, well, that's a topic for another day, I think." He sat on the worn leather couch and pulled at the heels of his work boots.

Tracy set the hiking boots in front of him and leaned back, arms crossed. When he didn't look at her, she stood and ambled to the curtainless bay windows—hips swaying invitingly.

He swallowed but his Adam's apple stuck halfway down his dry throat like a frozen engine piston.

"Sorry," she said. "I shouldn't be prying ... To tell you the truth

I've been a little off balance ever since I moved back. Can't seem to get my arms around the town or how I fit in anymore." She walked closer to the window. Sunlight from the kitchen caused a shimmering about her head, reminiscent of angel halos.

"What do they say? You can't go home." He'd lived in Palmer for most of his life and felt the same way. Maybe sometimes a man doesn't leave his home but home leaves him.

"Wow, that's depressing." She turned and this time he did hold her gaze.

Her amber eyes created a deep dark pool, sucking him into a world he had never considered. His fingers paused over the shoe laces and his lungs deflated. Time stood still. He breathed in deeply as a tingling spread behind his ears.

"Well, you know ... I mean, we're not in high school anymore ... We're not kids and both of us have been through a lot."

She moved closer. "I guess I was so intent on getting out of the military and Afghanistan, I never thought about what I'd be coming back to."

She smiled.

His heart fluttered.

"Helping out with the Christmas pageant does bring back some familiarity though, I have to say. I hope we'll still be able to have it. I don't think I ever remember a storm like this before Christmas."

Jake stood and placed a hand on her shoulder. "Somebody shot him, you know." His tongue reflexively wet his lower lip.

Jaw clenched. She stared steely-eyed up into his face. "Right. Saw enough of that in the Gulf. Chest shots, especially solo wounds, were well-positioned and intended kill shots." She stepped back, picked up Jake's box of shells. "I guess we should get to it ... Accuracy over takedown."

She pointed to the .270 Remington rifle.

Again the flush rose in his neck, different this time. "Hey, it's not like it's a .243. My dad bought this for me when I was fourteen. It'll do the job on most deer."

"Not much punch. A .270's only good to a couple hundred yards or so ... and on a man? Well, I don't know."

"Let's hope it doesn't come to that." Jake threw the fleece over his shoulder and pushed out through the ancient front door. They had a tough afternoon in store for them. Nonetheless, he'd have to give Tracy Aspen some serious thought once things settled down.

Crisp winter air filled his lungs as tension eased from his chest.

Chapter 8

Moran Ranch, South Dakota

He sure could blush in a heartbeat—kind of cute. It hadn't been that way in high school though. Maybe a scrawny sophomore didn't present much of a challenge to the star quarterback. Back then, Natalie Casper had been a permanent appendage to Jake's arm, any time or place. She'd even seen them, on occasion, around town after he'd gone down to Rapid City for college. Apparently, the split occurred sometime around when the newly minted ranger had his falling out with the Park Service. A lot had changed for Jake Moran a couple years back.

"We're gonna have to keep up a good pace," Jake said. "Otherwise we may be stuck on the ridge when the full force of this storm hits."

"Just what are we looking for? Shell casings ... maybe a cigarette butt with DNA on it?" Tracy cinched up her seatbelt as the old truck bounced over frozen ruts and hidden rocks.

Jake tossed a quick glance at her, closely followed by a severe jerk of the truck to the left off a snow-covered mound of buckthorn. "I think I'll be parking this ol' beast for the rest of the winter. Time to kick the dust off the Polaris snowmobile the Tanners left behind." He veered right, onto an open pasture, where the bumps and twists came intermittently. "I reckon the Sheriff is just trying to find anything he can before the whole area is covered with snow for the winter."

A brief flicker of sunshine from the snow reflected off Jake's blue eyes like the shimmer on a deep mountain lake, a Black Hill's lake—not the Hindu Kush. She recognized the strain in her chest and heaviness in her throat. The same she'd experienced so many years earlier when sitting next to him. It was different now. She was his equal. Not some giggling school girl—though her adolescent desires to rub her hands across his chest and nibble his delectable ear lobes had not faded. She crossed her legs.

Out the front window the rocky rim of the Black Hills, behind Mount Rushmore, crept into view. A patchwork of shade and bright sunlight raced across the projecting landscape of Ponderosa Pine and isolated stands of aspen and birch. "There's going to be a lot of snow blowing around." Tracy rolled the window down halfway for a better view. "We'll be exposed the whole way up, for anyone up on the rim or a hundred places down in the gulch … It'll take a little longer but I think posting a sentry every hundred yards or so to cover us would be smart. We could all take turns."

"Like in Afghanistan?" Jake's brow creased in a stern expression.

"Right." Her neck flushed with heat. "I was a nurse then … you know. The Marines were the ones posting up." She kept her gaze directed out the window. "It's not like I can't shoot though. My job was just different over there."

"Did you carry a weapon?"

"Yeah! It was a war zone. I was a legal target like everyone else." She smiled recalling her squad leader. "Sergeant Manny Hernandez always told me to stay put until the gunfire stopped. He said my job was to patch him up when he got shot. Not to get shot myself, 'cause then I'd be doin' nobody any good."

"How'd that work out?"

"We only lost one Marine from our squad, Tom Summers. A few guys got the Purple Heart for other things and two lost limbs. Even so, we were lucky." Heartache gripped her chest like a clenched fist and the rancid antiseptic smell of the triage tents assaulted her. She sighed. "There's no beauty in the Hindu Kush Mountains. It is nothing like here in the Black Hills." The stark contrast grated on her. "I don't know … sometimes—"

"Here's the Sheriff," Jake said. "It looks like he's got some help too."

She breathed deeply. A tremble crept down her spine. She rolled the window down all the way and gulped in the sweet, pure mountain air.

Jake eased his Ford truck between two sheriff's vehicles and a crime scene van. Technicians in khaki-colored jump suits and yellow parkas busied themselves cordoning off the outcropping of rocks at the trail head.

"That's where I found Stephen." Jake nodded toward the yellow crime scene tape, pulled his rifle from behind the driver's seat and closed the door. Tracy rolled up the window and retrieved her .30-06 from the bed of the truck.

Sheriff Schaffer stood with two deputies and a stocky technician studying a contour map stretched across the hood of a yellow and white crime scene vehicle.

"You see any activity up that way?" Tracy nodded toward the rim, dropped the lens covers from her rifle scope, and scanned the mountainous outcroppings, tall swaying pines, and the occasional line of spruce. Thankfully, the snow had lightened.

Schaffer scowled and shook his head. "Clay's been on it several times since we got here. We haven't seen anything."

The heavy-set deputy in full winter protective gear pulled a 7mm Remington magnum out of the backseat of the Sheriff's king cab truck. He likewise did a back and forth scan of the rapidly misting-over ridge line to the east, dropped his rifle simultaneously with Tracy. Both nodded.

Roger Hvinden, according to his name tag, plotted through the snow up to the Sheriff. "Found a recently fired bullet," he said. The lanky, mustached technician held a misshapen metal fragment in one of his white gloved hands, a metal detector in the other.

He placed his hand palm up on the hood of the truck as they all gathered around. Dirt and a little snow still clung to the deformed lump.

"The front's smashed but the base is still preserved," the Sheriff said.

Hvinden set the detector against the wheel-well of the truck and pointed to the base of the projectile. "I think you can make out some striations there, too." His mustache twitched to the right. "Probably a 165-grain, .30-06 pointed nose ... You get me the rifle and I think we can get a match."

Tracy swallowed hard. "165 ... A good mix of muzzle-velocity, trajectory, and takedown."

"Where'd you find it?" the Sheriff asked.

The technician slid the evidence into a zip-lock bag. He pointed to where two others were holding measuring sticks and taking pictures. "Right at the base of the rock where the boy was found."

"Thanks, Roger," the Sheriff said and nodded. "I don't suspect you'll find much more but give it a good once over."

Hvinden saluted as he ambled back toward the crime scene.

The Sheriff pulled a shotgun from a slot in his dash. "Miss Aspen, you ready to go?"

"We can go up the trail here," she said. "But the easier approach to the summit is up from east of the Kincaid ranch, on park land, just off the forest road at the entrance to the gulch." She pointed to a distant peak to the northeast. "I'd suggest we come down that way if you can arrange a pick-up, Sheriff. That's probably where a shooter would've come in from."

"Right, might be some tire tracks we could get some impressions of." The Sheriff did a quick survey of his personnel. "Clay, have Ned or someone from forensics get another unit over to the northwest end of Boxelder, and have them tread lightly. We're gonna need all the evidence we can find." He glanced at Jake and over toward Tracy like he was going to say something, but then abruptly turned and walked back to his truck. He opened a back door and pulled gloves and a fur-flapped hat off the rear seat.

Tracy picked her way around the yellow-clad technicians. Her hiking boots bit firmly through the dusting of snow. Cold dry gravel crunched with each step. Here and there a resilient stalk of showy sedge poked up. "I'll move up the incline a hundred yards or so and post. That'll give an elevated view of the gulch. Sun'll be at our backs … That's always good." She chambered a round and checked her safety. "Come on up when you're ready. But remember—we're burnin' daylight here—sunset is 3:45."

The Sheriff nodded and spit a chew of tobacco downwind toward Jake's fence line.

Pine needles underfoot crackled and filled the air with the crisp fragrance of pine and freshly fallen snow. Fifty yards up the trail Tracy turned to find Jake tight on her heels. His steady breaths caused a glistening of moisture to condense on his light beard. They'd be icicles before the group reached the crest. Under the hood of his parka, he wore a gun-metal gray stocking cap as added protection against the cold.

"Shooting down into a ravine is a tricky shot." She spoke evenly between deep inhalations, as she climbed steadily up the rocky trail. "It messes with the trajectory-drop pretty dramatically after a couple hundred yards. Whoever shot Stephen knew what they were doing and where they wanted the bullet to hit."

Jake caught up to her as she stopped just after the third switch-back. "Combat experience or hunting with your dad?"

Tracy glanced over Jake's back. The Sheriff and his deputies talking and waving hands had started up the trail. She shouldered her rifle and sighted the ridge above them, then swung a lazy arch along Boxelder Gulch. "A little of both, I guess," she mumbled into the stock of the rifle. Satisfied, she lowered the weapon. "Like I said, I didn't really do the shooting over there."

Jake exhaled deeply and with hands on his knees stared at her through penetrating blue eyes.

•

He prided himself on being able to hike all day with a fifty-pound pack, more if necessary. He'd always been one of the strongest in the Park Corps. Tracy could probably do the same. He regretted his failure at getting to know her—self-reliant, athletic, driven. Natalie would have never been caught in camouflaged gear climbing to a wilderness ridge line, toting a hunting rifle.

He had never complained about her choice of clothes though, she was just different from Tracy. And, certainly knew her way around the Mall of the Americas in Minneapolis.

"Still clear," Tracy said as she surveyed the darkening shadows below the south summit for the fourth time in a quarter mile.

Above them the clouds accelerated as they passed over the crest to the southeast. The fine mist collected on Jake's thin beard.

Tracy glanced back down at the struggling deputy, who carried an extra thirty pounds around the mid-section. She winked at Jake. "I'll move up to that granite outcropping to the east ... Take your time moving up the trail. I'll be able to catch any movement on the ridge or in the gulch from that vantage."

Sheriff Schaffer pushed his Stetson back on his head and wiped his brow with a paisley handkerchief. Tracy smiled at Jake as she swung her athlete hips and briskly started up the final incline to the observation site.

"Hold your horses, missy." The Sheriff shoved the handkerchief in a pocket above the fur-lined hat hanging from his belt. The corner of his mouth twitched. He glanced above her and then down the incline toward the crime scene crew.

Tracy bent low to reduce her target profile. Jake flashed to that kneeling profile and the football game where he'd torn the ligament in his knee. She'd been there on the sideline with him that day, saying nothing but there right up to when they'd loaded him into the back of the coach's truck and left for the hospital.

The past ten years had brought changes to his life that had left him drained and disenchanted. He could have easily turned to the bottle as did some of his friends. Fortunately he'd resisted at every heartbreaking and painful turn of misfortune. What sorrow pulled at Tracy's heart? She had an easy smile yet her gaze held a depth beyond her years—not so much a sadness as a deep and profound remorse.

Chapter 9

Western edge of Boxelder Gulch

There! A flash in the gulch. Tracy's gaze snapped to the left instinctively.

"What?" Jake glanced back down the trail, to the law enforcement officers struggling the last hundred yards to the crest, slipping on snow and loose gravel.

Tracy wrapped her arm around his denim jacket. Taut, hard muscles resisted her pull. Still she swung both of them behind the table rock she'd been using to steady her rifle. She put a finger over her lips. "Shhh." She glanced down the trail and west along the gulch toward the Kincaid Ranch ... lazy moving needle-grass, a grove of juniper buffeted by the wind.

She'd seen it though. She was sure. An unnatural movement, a glimmer of light, birds suddenly stirred. This time it was a reflection from the gulch just as she'd lowered her rifle sight. Jake's gaze held hers with a perplexed but receptive knit to his brow. "Someone is across the gulch watching us." She leaned in close and whispered, "Get the Sheriff and his deputy up behind the outcropping without arousing them."

Jake nodded and eased down on his knees as he peered around the boulder shielding them from below. She heard a muted, "Psst. Psst." The rest must have been hand motions. She slowly eased the .30-06 up on the flat rock surface and focused her scope on the western side of Boxelder Gulch. Nothing. At least nothing yet.

A glance to her left revealed Jake whispering to the Sheriff and deputy. All three checked their weapons. Tracy again swept the short arch required to survey the dusty rock-strewn far bank of the gulch—pine and juniper shrubs, bull thistle and buckthorn. Nothing moving. She motioned to Jake and pointed at a dry sagebrush next to him. He handed it up and Tracy quickly flattened it over the rifle barrel and scope.

The moist aroma of dirt and pine mixed with a whiff of crushed sage. A couple vesper sparrows flirted about a stand of buckthorn at the near end of the gulch. Wind whipped through amber-colored Oatgrass—nothing unnatural. She slowed her breathing. The pounding in her chest eased and settled into a hunter's rhythm.

Again ... A movement followed by a dull cloud-reflected flash. And then just as quickly two flicks of light. Someone with binoculars or a rifle scope was sweeping their position. The puff of smoke registered just as the tumble bush shuddered and stone exploded behind her. Her finger on the trigger guard instinctively engaged as the warm air in her lungs slowly exhaled into her hand, gripped around the rifle stock. A flash from her muzzle and her right hand flew through the bolt action, once—twice—three times. Though she'd only had to do it twice while deployed, the instincts came back in a rush. The caustic taste of burned sulfur touched her mouth.

"What the hell!" The deputy flipped his hat on the ground and bent to peer around the boulder.

The Sheriff pulled back on the deputy's shoulder. "Time to keep your squash down, lad ... two hundred yards at a stationary target is not a difficult shot."

Jake leaned his back against the boulder and released the safety on his rifle as did the Sheriff on his shot gun. Tracy showed them two fingers and a thumb ... closed her fist and began opening them, thumb first. On three, Jake and the Sheriff aimed around the boulder and shot blindly toward the gulch and away from the crime scene technicians. Tracy swung back onto the table rock as a round ricocheted somewhere above them. Amazing how accuracy drops off when someone is shooting back at you.

A brown jacket and black hair disappeared over the rocky bank as fast as they appeared. Tracy let fly two more shots with a prayer, knowing damn well the assailant had moved out of sight line. "He's running ... back toward the north trailhead if we're real lucky."

The Sheriff barked orders into his handheld radio. He turned grimacing and shook his head. "They won't be to the parking lot for another twenty minutes … and there're at least six forest and ranch roads that lead into that area." He stared up to the darkening sky and swatted at the plump falling snow flakes. "I don't have enough personnel to cover half of those roads, even if we had a map handy and could figure the best intercepts."

Tracy pulled a box of bullets out of her jacket pocket and re-loaded. The Sheriff popped the breech on his shot gun. Jake rubbed two dirty fingers across his lips as he chewed on the lower one.

Her breaths came in deep sighs. The moist hairs on the back of her neck began to relax. "I thought I'd left all of that in Afghani-stan." She half smiled at the men. "We better get done what we have to do up here and clear out before they've a chance to regroup." She aimed the barrel of her rifle to the west. "I only caught sight of one. Might be more … Only one shooting though."

The Sheriff nodded. "Hard to tell."

He and Deputy Caulfield spent the next few minutes on the radio coordinating possible intercepts and warning everyone to consider anyone on those roads armed and dangerous.

Tracy pointed up the ridge trail. "I can only think of two maybe three sites to post up here and have a clear shot into the gulch." She sat back against the rock and rested the .30-06 across her shoulder, hands warming in her armpits. "If you'll keep an eye on things here Jake, I'll walk the Sheriff up and settle myself above them until they've finished their work." Tight-jawed, his stare held resolve, like she'd seen in the Special Forces soldiers. Maybe she'd underestimated him.

He ejected the spent cartridge and chambered a new one. "Let's get a move on. I don't want to be on this mountainside with a target taped on my back any longer than necessary."

Several rock spires gave them partial cover as they moved up the trail. Within ten minutes, she'd shown the Sheriff the three sites. He rejected the first right off—assigned the deputy to the second one and set to work on the remaining site just below where Tracy posted. She continually swept the far crest as well as Box-elder Gulch. Nothing for now.

She could just make out Jake in the waning light from the dark storm clouds and murkiness of intermittent flurries. He'd certainly shown his mettle today. Being a football hero was nothing like challenges faced by troops overseas or the lawmen who put their lives on the line daily. Turned out though that the old gridiron hero had all the right stuff. So what had happened with the Park Service?

•

Jake studied the haze shrouded landscape from his perch as Deputy Caulfield methodically searched the ground around the outcropping. Within a minute or so of taking up his position he picked up the barely discernible pop of a motorbike, two-cycle engine from somewhere up Boxelder Gulch.

The last time he'd been shot at had been on an investigation up east of Spearfish Canyon nearly four years earlier. A large track of National Forest ran between two limestone cliffs for nearly fifty miles up into North Dakota. Two sets of backpackers had gone missing over the summer and the only sign was a bloodied backpack found wedged under a stand of spruce just off the Yakima Wilderness Trail, more than ten miles in.

Due to the interstate implications the FBI had been called in, the lead agent fervently announcing who was in charge. Shortly after the Feds arrived the faint hum of a low-flying airplane had preceded multiple gunshots from high up on the western ridge line. It was doubtful that even a high-powered rifle could reach the law enforcement team from that distance and it had been unclear to Jake if there was a connection or not to the missing hikers.

Though first on the scene, he and the other Park Rangers had been summarily dismissed once the FBI was able to enlist the aid of the Lawrence County Sheriff and his force of four-wheel-drive vehicles.

When Jake had left the Park Service two years later, to his knowledge, nothing had ever been resolved. Family members of the missing hikers had contacted the Park Service initially but in the end it was a FBI investigation. Jake had been invited to "keep his nose out of" the incident.

Tracy and the Sheriff picked their way down from the upper rock ledge. The Sheriff still wore his Stetson cowboy hat—fur-lined cap tucked in his belt as a talisman against further deterioration of the weather. "That was just about worthless," he said. "Had to be done though … and obviously somebody doesn't want us up here."

"It doesn't make any sense," Tracy said.

"A lot of times it doesn't." The Sheriff studied the corroded and tarnished bullet-casing that Caulfield handed him. "Nothing's been shot from this shell in years ... bag it though."

"I heard a motorcycle up the gulch toward the Kincaids' a little while back," Jake said.

The Sheriff nodded toward Caulfield. "Let everyone know to keep their eyes out. That's about the only way to get in and out of that gulch, I'd think."

While Caulfield thumbed the radio Jake stood behind the rock outcropping with the Sheriff and Tracy. "Anything new on Stephen Kincaid since last night?"

The Sheriff glanced at his deputy. "Did you think Clint Kincaid was holding something back?"

"When you told him about Stephen last night?"

"Yeah, it was like he wasn't that surprised to hear about the shooting." The Sheriff brushed snow off his coat shoulders. "I don't know ... I've never had much dealings with Clint."

Jake rechecked the safety on his rifle. "You know what else was odd," he said. "There was a Koran next to Stephen's bed but a lighted cross and Christmas lights on the Kincaids' house ... And just as we left Clint turned them off, like them being on might've meant something."

"His parents said he was home for Christmas." The Sheriff shifted his shotgun to the other hand. "Up in Canada, you said. College?"

"Toronto, I heard." A dusting of snow whipped off the rock ledge and pelted the three of them. "I don't recall anything about college though ... in fact I don't remember Clint saying anything about Stephen leaving except that he'd gone up into Canada—and that was all."

"I'll be visiting with Clint again tomorrow," the Sheriff said.

"Anything come of Stephen's computer?" Jake asked.

The Sheriff shook his head. "Haven't been able to have anyone look at it ... and with this storm. It may be next week before I can get it over to Rapid City."

"Cat could take a crack at it," Tracy said.

"Yeah, she's a whiz at computers." Jake smiled. "She's not just a pretty face and a great cook. Computer science was her major."

"Right, well this is a murder investigation," the Sheriff puffed. "I don't want to contaminate the evidence. I've had about all the fun I can have in one day. Let's get off this damn mountain."

"Leads will be pretty cold by next week." Tracy slipped past Caulfield and started down the trail. "Catherine could do it at the Sheriff's station with you watching her every move."

Jake watched the sway of her hips as she maneuvered on the slippery snow cover trail.

The Sheriff glanced between the two of them. "Damn Canadian storms. Nobody kills someone in the middle of a snow storm ... unless they've got a darn good reason for doin' it."

A scurrying marmot gave them all a scare halfway down from the rim. Jake laughed at Tracy who threw herself on the ground, rifle at the ready. "You huntin' for dinner now?" He chuckled.

"That might be all I have for Christmas if I don't get off this mountain and to the grocery store sometime tonight."

Jake helped her up from the ground. His large hand nearly encircled her upper arm. She really was a slim, trim, fighting machine. He swatted dirt and snow from her pants and felt a quiver up into his neck. He wanted to touch her more.

"What goes with varmint Christmas dinner anyway?" She smiled, straight white teeth and those adorable dimples. Multicolored Christmas lights danced in her eyes.

Jake's stomach flipped like a kid doing a cartwheel.

"I guess Cranberry Bush or Sweet Arrowleaf would be best." The Sheriff laughed. "You'd be surprised what my grandmother used to cook up ... Why I remember—"

The radio on his hip crackled with static. A weak voice faded in and out and then steadied more clearly. "Sheriff Schaffer, over."

He keyed the radio. "Schaffer here, go ahead." He released the key. "It's Stan at dispatch," he said.

"We got some visitors, Sheriff." Static briefly broke through before the Sheriff adjusted a few small nobs. "They're requesting you bring Jake back to the station with you, over."

The Sheriff abandoned radio protocol. "You're breaking up, Stan. Who's they?"

The group stood in the shelter of Ponderosa Pines and watched, through a break in the snowfall, billowing clouds attack the summit behind Mount Rushmore.

Jake's stomach went from a flutter to a sinking sensation, like a mixer jumping from blend to whip.

The Sheriff repeated his question into the handheld radio, "Who are the visitors, Stan?"

"FBI."

Jake rubbed his hand across the back of his neck and studied the Sheriff.

•

What the hell was Jake into? Tracy searched her mind for what she'd been told about his dismissal from the Ranger Service. There had been a death associated with that incident also. Nothing illegal had been mentioned though. Hard to believe he'd be involved in anything like that. Still she hadn't pressed the issue with anyone. She really didn't know, and a lot could change in ten years.

The crime scene crew, after conferring with Sheriff Schafer, decided to shift their evidence samples and the investigation to Rapid City, if they could beat the storm—much more forensic equipment than in Palmer.

"Trace, you can ride with me and Clay or with Jake," the Sheriff said. "Your choice ... Clay can take the backseat."

The burly deputy shuffled his feet a bit and glanced at the Sheriff. Clearly, the two-hundred-and-thirty-plus lawman did not relish riding in the back seat.

She slapped the officer on the back. "No, I'll ride with the 'help.' At least his heater works."

"Sometimes," Jake said.

They rode in silence across the pasture and cut behind the homestead toward the south gate. The cab of the truck smelled of stale hay and musty cattle ... home.

She watched Jake, almost expecting him to be chewing on a shaft of straw. His lip was getting the action, no straw.

"What's it all about?" She broke the silence.

"The FBI you mean?"

"Yeah, why does the FBI need to talk with you ... if I'm not prying too much?" She turned on the truck's bench seat to better face him.

Jake coaxed the old pickup down the icy road toward Palmer, snow slithered off the front window. The windshield wipers fought a losing battle with snow and ice accumulation. He glanced in her direction—an uncharacteristic twitch at the corner of his eye.

"Does this have to do with why you left the Ranger Service? Or with the militia?"

"What?" He held his mouth tightly and shook his head. "That was all over deviations from Service protocols … nothing illegal." His brow knitted. "Is that what you were thinking?"

"Sorry, I didn't know." Tracy swallowed hard, turned her head and listened to the snow slap and splatter against the fenders of the truck. "I've only heard a few things at the hospital. I guess it was kinda old news."

Jake stared into the oncoming storm. "Look, I'm trying to move on." He glanced at Tracy. His chin tipped up and his nostrils flared. He shook his head nearly imperceptibly. He owed no one an explanation.

She reached her hand to his arm, the tension in the muscles palpable. "Jake, I'm glad we had a chance to meet again after all these years." She swallowed hard, tears fighting to flood down her cheek.

He took his left hand off the steering wheel and tenderly placed it over hers on his arm. He blinked several times and exhaled slowly. "So am I, Trace … We've both had some hard years." He chewed lightly on his lower lip just before a slight grin edged the side of his mouth. "Those are behind us though. This shooting will pass too and then … well, we'll see. I hope anyway." He turned more fully toward her as she steadfastly refused to let a tear sneak out.

She smiled back, removed her hand, and slugged him gently on the shoulder. "Oh, we will, will we?" She tilted her chin slightly and considered the Jake she had never really seen before. "Sounds to me like a cowboy wishing for some really big things for Christmas."

"A new furnace would be a good start," he half mumbled while holding back a chuckle.

Tracy flipped her hair over her left shoulder and picked a burr from her camouflaged slacks. "So, the FBI must want to talk with you about the shooting."

"Yeah, and why would they be involved with a local murder?" His fingers played along that inviting lower lip.

What would it taste and feel like to nibble that lip again? She'd wondered that for a decade. "They were at our base in Afghanistan—always investigating something."

"That's different though. You were out of the country. Here in South Dakota, murder is a state offense."

"Clearly then there's more to it, something crossing state lines or a kidnapping." Tracy slipped her arms out of her coat as the heater kicked in. Jake did a double-take on her chest as she arched her back to slip the coat onto the seat next to her. She leered at him but his concentration was already back on the road.

"Has to be somethin' like that," Jake said. "Maybe they've had other shootings, like over in Wyoming. That would put it 'cross state lines and make it a federal case."

Tracy rubbed her chin. Something wasn't right about Stephen Kincaid. He had bled much more freely than the casualties she'd worked on in Helmand. And what about his lab results? They were also odd. The print-out from the hospital computer was still stuck in her bag in the bed of the truck.

"I'll drop you off before going to the Sheriff's station." Jake down shifted as they approached town.

"Isn't the station just up Bighorn Way?"

"Yeah, it is."

"Well, that's ridiculous. You'd have to go all the way through town and back to drop me off." She wiped frost from the passenger-side window as Christmas decorations appeared at scattered home sites.

"I don't know how long I'll be with the Sheriff and the Feds."

"I'm fine," she said. "Los Arbolitos is just up the hill from the station ... I can always hike up the road for dinner, if it's gonna take a long time."

"Hey." Jake nodded. "That's a deal. And I'll buy if I can shake free quick enough." His eyes twinkled when he glanced at her.

Or, maybe she'd just caught a reflection of the Christmas ornaments.

"A date with the high school quarterback?" Tracy giggled.

"Right." His sandy-blond hair bounced as he shook his head and smirked.

Cute.

Chapter 10

Pennington County Sheriff's Station, Palmer

Steam wafted off the engine compartment of the blue and white Homeland Security helicopter that sat conspicuously in the Sheriff's station parking lot. Blowing snow nearly covered several trails of footprints leading from the empty, silent helicopter to the double-glass doors of the administrative building. Scattered meticulously trimmed holly bushes bordered the single-story heavily windowed, brick building.

Two large, black SUVs sat near the flagpole at the front entrance—also empty. The American flag, along with the state flag of South Dakota and a MIA flag, stood straight out from the pole, the ends brutally shaken by the excessive wind. Tracy had seen these black SUVs often in Afghanistan. Bad news.

"Holy cow, this isn't just the FBI," she said. "They send an agent or two, not a whole contingent complete with air support."

Jake eased the truck to a stop at the opposite end of the parking lot. "Something's up." Hand gripping the steering wheel he stared icily at the entrance to the Sheriff's Station. "This could get dicey ... no telling what they're cookin' up at their little conference."

"Yeah, and I have to tell you." The skin on her forehead tightened. "I've never known any guys driving those SUVs who had a sense of humor."

"I can still drive you to your apartment and then come back alone ... If you're afraid."

"Jerk," she said. "And here I thought you'd grown up a little in the past decade."

"Ouch! Let me say that I'm sure this experience will be much more pleasurable with you at my side."

Tracy pulled a hair barrette from her coat pocket and pinned her bangs tightly on the left side. She studied her profile in a visor mirror. "Don't they say the best defense is a good offense?"

"What are you suggesting?"

"We go in guns blazing," she said. "What's going on? Why is someone shooting and killing ranchers east of town? Who's in charge?"

Jake stroked the stubble on his chin as he stared at the flapping flags. "I'll take it under advisement. Let me take the lead though, if it's okay with you?"

"Whatever, it's your skin. I'll play the silent supportive woman." She smiled and opened the truck door. Snow swirled about in the halogen lights which had cycled on with the gloom of the afternoon. Cold snaked down her blouse and goosebumps attacked her neck as she quickly slid on her coat and gloves.

Gusting, stabbing wind drowned out the crunch of their feet in the snow. The protected entrance alcove gave a welcome respite. Jake held the door for her.

Sheriff Schaffer and his deputy, the portly Clay Caulfield, had parked in the back of the station. They were already talking with two men in suits and a third man, clean-shaven and nearly Jake's height, dressed in hunting attire.

"Carl," Jake said as he approached the group.

"Jake, thanks for coming in." The tall hunter reached a well-manicured hand to Jake and nodded to Tracy. Jake hesitantly returned the handshake.

"Ma'am, I'm Carl Atwood with the South Dakota FBI."

Tracy offered her hand and the agent shook it as well.

Atwood introduced them to the other agents, both from Homeland Security out of Omaha. Both stood nearly as tall as Atwood, wore dark suits with button-down shirts and nondescript ties. The Sheriff motioned the group to a conference room where Deputy Caulfield and a female dispatcher where spreading coffee cups. Metal-framed, brown plastic-backed chairs lined each wall and surrounded the wood-laminate conference table. Tracy and Jake pulled off their coats. Holding the coffee in both hands she let the heat creep into her sore fingers.

The helicopter pilot and two other agents or officers loitered about the waiting room watching the weather channel chart the progress of the Canadian storm. One of the men wore what resembled an Air Force flight suit but had no identifiable insignia.

"The kid they brought in was your neighbor?" Carl Atwood asked Jake. "The Kincaid boy?"

Jake folded his coat and set it in a chair against the wall. At the end of the table the two Homeland agents flipped through data screens on an iPad. Jake pulled a chair out for Tracy and also sat down. Atwood continued to stand until Jake motioned for him to sit down.

"What's going on, Carl?" Jake studied the slim middle-aged agent. "Look … I'm not with the Park Service anymore. I'm a civilian. If you want cooperation you need to let us know what we're getting into."

Atwood glanced at the occupied Homeland officers. He rubbed both hands through his short brown hair, sat down, and took a long swig of coffee. "It's complicated," he said.

"That's all we get?" Jake held Atwood's gaze.

He grimaced. "For now. Let's hear what you got."

"Okay." Jake glanced at Tracy. "So, let's see." He kneaded the facial hair on his chin, studied the coffee cup and shook his head slightly. "I found Stephen shot up by Horse Thief Ridge and brought him to the emergency room yesterday morning."

"He was pretty much gone when we got him," Tracy said.

Carl Atwood stared at Tracy, one eyebrow raised.

"I'm the emergency department charge nurse," she said.

"And why were you on the mountain this afternoon?" the agent asked.

Jake and Tracy proceeded to explain their acquaintance from high school and her experience hunting the Horse Thief area with her father. Atwood made short cryptic notes in a steno pad. When he pressed Jake on specifics, penetrating stares and barely visible snarls flared on both rugged Dakotans.

Sheriff Schaffer came out of a side office, swung his leg over a backward chair, and sat down across from Atwood. The testosterone battle abated. Schaffer helped fill in some of the events from earlier in the day as Jake's answers deteriorated to "yes" and "no." The agent seemed cordial to the Sheriff and smiled brightly, even joking a bit. He asked Tracy for clarification on time of death and a few particulars about the resuscitation attempts.

"Sounds like you guys at the hospital pulled out all the stops."

Carl Atwood patted her arm. "It takes a special dedication to dig into the bloody carnage and devastation that gun battles wreak." His stylish hunting shirt sported a crisp press.

Atwood's haircut and shave presented sharp well-trimmed lines. His short, gelled hair sprouted just a smattering of grey, rather distinguished actually. He leaned in close. Tracy's heartbeat jumped into her neck. She breathed deeply to prevent a flush.

Jake exhaled slowly. "Okay, Carl." He folded his hands on the table and squared off with the federal agent. "What is going on ... beyond the murder of young Kincaid?"

"Drones," the Sheriff said. He glanced toward the Homeland agents who had been joined by the man in a flight suit. All three studied a topographical map of the Black Hills Region and Mount Rushmore.

"Damn, Sheriff." Atwood's face turned red and a grimace showed clenched teeth. "That's departmental intel ... Not for released to civilians."

"Yeah, right." The Sheriff scoffed at Atwood. "If you want to get in and out of that area you're gonna need the help of these civilians."

Atwood sat back and put a thumb in his belt. "Not a word to the press." A spark ignited in his hazel eyes as they jumped between Tracy and Jake. "Not even to your families ... nothing."

"What about drones over the Black Hills?" Jake asked.

Tracy sat back, fingers to her lips.

The Sheriff stared at Agent Atwood, who leaned forward in his chair and characteristically looked left and right. "Well, a bit more is in play than just drone over-flights, I'm afraid." He checked the Homeland Security officers who were still occupied examining data feed to their iPhones and iPads. "Radiation surveillance has detected likely weapons-quality emissions from the area below Horse Thief Ridge."

"Honestly." The Sheriff opened his hands on the table. "I just found out about this myself. We're still investigating the killing. And, sorry to say, the team wants to examine the body—tonight."

"Wait a minute," Jake said. A flush crossed his ears. "Do you mean the drones detected a radiation signature near my ranch?"

The Sheriff weakly gestured at Agent Atwood.

"We're not saying anything about over-flight surveillance." Atwood scowled at the Sheriff. "Don't read more into this than there is … just 'cause Major Crews is here should not lead to any drone speculation."

"That's a bunch of crap!" Jake crumpled the paper coffee cup.

"Just assume for now," Atwood said, "that the radiation we're talking about was detected in some way via a rail or land portal monitor."

"Whatever," Jake said. "Is it still up there … Boxelder Gulch or up on Horse Thief?"

"They've lost the signal," the Sheriff said. "That's why they've all shown up here."

Atwood stood and finished his coffee. "And Palmer will be crawling with Feds if we don't get answers soon."

"And somehow you think the killing of Stephen Kincaid yesterday is related to all this?" Jake asked.

Atwood twisted his head toward the Sheriff. "The kid was shot yesterday?"

"Probably right around sunrise," the Sheriff said. "As best we can determine."

Atwood pushed his chair back and tapped on the observation window. He waved a finger at the flight-suited Major who met him outside the conference room door. Atwood pointed at the pilot's iPad and spoke in a low, unrecognizable tone. The military office shook his head two or three times and then shrugged his shoulders.

Atwood stepped back into the room and stared for a moment at Jake. "You're sure he was shot yesterday morning?"

Tracy answered. "No one could survive that wound more than a few hours."

"I was asking Jake," Atwood said tersely.

"Ask the Sheriff," Jake said. "His parents told us he'd been home sick the night before."

"You've been out to his house?" Atwood shifted his attack to Sheriff Schafer.

"Christ, Carl." The Sheriff finished his coffee. "You're trying awfully hard to fit this murder into some screwed up time line, it seems to me."

Atwood pursed his lips twice. He glared hard at each of them individually. Probably trying to decide who was lying or holding something back. He fixed on Jake but then backed off when Jake stared him down.

He focused instead on Tracy's chest. "Can you help us get to that body, Ma'am?"

What the hell was going on? Of course, in her military training Tracy had extensive exposure to detection devices, chemical, biological, and nuclear. Her emergency triage courses had drilled her on in field mitigation actions and assessment, not any kind of capability the local authorities in Palmer would have. Why should they?

"He's likely still in the hospital morgue. I know the plan was to send the body to the crime lab in Rapid City. That probably won't happen till tomorrow though." She nodded toward Schaffer. "I would think it's the Sheriff's call as to who gets access to the body, especially before any formal autopsy."

"Yeah, damn," the Sheriff said. "I think it's pretty safe to say this whole affair has been kicked upstairs." He ran thick, knotted fingers through his salt-and-pepper hair. "Gi'me an hour or two to get one of the lab techs from Rapid City up here so we can protect the chain-of-custody 'n all that crap."

Carl Atwood eased Tracy's chair out for her. "Fine," he said. "In the meantime, can we drive down to the hospital and go over what you found during Stephen Kincaid's time in the emergency room?"

As she stood, Atwood rested his hand on her upper arm. It felt constricting, restraining even. An uneasy smile pulled at the edges of her mouth as she confronted his cold stare. He smiled, a debonair "lady killer" smile. The kind she'd seen before in military officer's clubs.

·

Jake pulled the collar up on his camouflaged coat as the group step out into the Dakota winter. Atwood was up to his old lady-chasing tricks. Natalie had fallen hard for the suave federal agent a few years back, enough so to introduce her older cousin to the athletic divorcee. Jake knew little of how the relationship had ended, just like he'd never found out from Atwood what had happened to the missing backpackers in Spearfish Canyon … or if the Feds had anything to do with Bret Peterson's posting to South Dakota.

Tracy could take care of herself. She wasn't the skinny kid who'd been all, "Hey, Jake," giggles and, "Oh, golly." She had been brave enough to go-for-it-all in the hay loft that night. He could still remember the pale softness of her breasts, her heaving chest. It had been a crazy year, a year when his world literally crumbled around him.

She'd recovered enough from his rejection to give him a sweet kiss on the cheek at graduation. How much improved would her kisses be after all these years? He'd actually been pretty impressed even back then, a genuine kiss, honest and bestowed freely. Even at eighteen, he'd known it meant more than any kiss from Natalie.

The temperature had dropped several degrees as had the force of the wind. Tracy wrapped her scarf around her neck as the trio watched the Homeland Security contingent load into one of the dark SUVs. Atwood walked her to the remaining SUV and helped her into the passenger's seat as he simultaneously examined her derriere. Jerk.

"Carl, you need me to come down to the hospital, too?" Jake felt like a third wheel interfering on some adolescent date.

"Probably so," Atwood said. "Might need to review what happened before you got to the hospital." He smiled again at Tracy. Closed the side door and approached Jake at the front of the SUV. "The kid say anything to you when you first found him?"

Jake rubbed the stubble on his chin. "I wasn't even sure if he was alive or dead, at first." His fingers pulled at the edges of his mouth. "Though I could feel a weak pulse and thought at the time he was breathing a little."

"What did you do once you got him to the hospital?"

"They were pretty shorthanded in the emergency room so I stuck around and helped with the resuscitation."

"Really." Atwood raised his eyebrows and glared at Jake, who'd glanced through the window at Tracy. "She your girlfriend ... or something?"

His scalp tingled and a heat ran up his neck into his ears. "No—not really. A little high school thing—years ago." Atwood was like a tomcat spraying his scent in every ally. Jake would have loved to just smash the guy in his leering face.

"I guess I could see doin' a little chest pounding and lip-locking with that pretty lady," Atwood said facing away from Tracy, rub-bing his gloved hand across his mouth.

Jake tried not to react to the crude agent. He nodded at Tracy through the SUV window. "I'll see you at the hospital, Carl. Drive carefully. It's getting really slick out there. I don't want to be havin' to pull you out of a ditch."

"Don't you worry, Ranger." Atwood smirked and popped a breath mint in his mouth. "One way or another I'll keep that little filly warm."

Jake kicked the accumulating snow as he walked across the parking lot to his truck. He hit the ignition and lights. The SUV had not moved. He waited for it to pass. Intent on follow them to the hospital. What was an FBI agent going to do to a witness on a dark, freezing South Dakota road?

He didn't trust Atwood, who'd been the lead on the Spearfish Canyon investigation. Jake regretted that he'd never been able to give the families closure on their loved ones. He'd pushed Atwood to share the FBI evidence, even going over his head at one time with an email to the Executive Deputy Assistant for National Security. That had resulted in a standard reply. "The matter is being investigated at the state level. Notification of findings will be forwarded to the National Park Service from The South Dakota office as developments occur." In other words—"kiss off."

All that had taken a back seat to the events of Bret Peterson's accidental death, the incident that ultimately resulted in Jake's dismissal. The two or three times he and his attorney had attempted to subpoena records as to why Peterson was detailed to Mount Rushmore in the first place resulted in doors being slammed in their faces—"National Security Restricted Access."

His cell phone rang. Watching the icy conditions he carefully pushed receive.

"Jake ... It's Tracy."

His heart thumped in his chest. "I'm right behind you." He gripped the steering wheel tightly, willed himself to take a deep breath.

"Yeah, I can see," she said. "Since our date is ruined I thought I'd call ahead for some hospital chow to be delivered to the ER."

"Your treat?"

"Heck no, I'll charge it to the federal government." He heard a snicker over the phone. "Agent Atwood says he'll pick up the tab for both of us ... such a deal."

He briefly told her what he liked and didn't like wondering all along what Carl Atwood thought about her date comment. A blanket of snow covered the roadside needle grass and occasional bull thistle shrub as they turned up the hill toward the well-lighted hospital.

Thinking of Tracy and Carl Atwood left a sour taste in the back of his throat and a burning sensation in his gut.

Chapter 11

Patriot's Hospital

Carl Atwood fancied himself a "player." How that mixed with being a senior FBI agent mulled about in Tracy's mind as she poured water from the cooler into three paper cups for her and the two hormonal adolescents faced off in front of her.

"Food'll be here in fifteen minutes," she said, handing cups to the two men.

Jake paced back and forth across the trauma bay. Atwood stretched his neck side to side, paging through his notes.

"So, where do you think the radiation source is now?" Jake bit his lip and rubbed his three-day growth of beard. Bright blue eyes studied the federal agent.

"That's the ten-thousand-dollar question … and it's why we're here." Atwood unlatched a padded camera-like bag he'd carried into the emergency room. He pointed to a white sheet-covered gurney. "This is where you worked on him?"

"Right here where the cardiac monitors and suction equipment are." She put her hand on a stretcher against the wall, bent and picked up a stray needle cap resting next to the gurney. "I don't know if this was the stretcher he was on though … We pretty much move them around depending on if the patient has been over to X-ray or into surgery. Once the patients are back and discharged, Sam Whitcomb sanitizes the beds and lines them down the hallway or puts them in an empty bay."

Atwood examined the trauma room, finally absently focusing on the large cylindrical light mounted from the ceiling. "So, he didn't leave here until they took him to the morgue?"

Tracy flipped through a loose-leaf folder with several colored tabs. "The resuscitation records said he was pronounced forty-two minutes after Jake crashed into the entrance door. He was here, in the trauma bay, that whole time."

Atwood toggled a switch and walked about the room waving a sensor probe attached by a cord to, what Tracy assumed was, a Geiger counter. The machine made a low-pitched purr and nothing else. The deflection needle on the black Tech 93m held steady. His face scrunched up as he shifted his gaze about the corners of the medical treatment room. "Nothing ... Where are his clothes?"

"They'd be in the morgue," Tracy said. "With the body."

"Okay, so he came in through the emergency doors and right to this trauma room, right?" Atwood leaned out the wide door and into the hallway. "Can you give me a brief overview of how everything went?"

"Sure." Tracy lay the chart on the gurney and selected three sheets of paper. "Code red started at 8:48 initiated by me." She continued chronologically through the sheets.

Holding up a hand, Atwood said. "Whoa! How much blood did you give him?"

"Six units and some fresh frozen plasma," Tracy said. She tapped her hand on the middle sheet. "We drew blood early on, as is typical for any code ... The peculiar thing about the Kincaid kid was, he just would not clot."

"That's not what you usually see with a gunshot wound, is it?" Atwood peered over her shoulder at the medical records.

She recognized his cologne, Obsession, one of her favorites. He stood close, his thigh resting against her hip. Heat flared up the base of her neck, and it wasn't his warm breath. She held still. The pressure against her thigh increased. She glanced back at him. He smiled but did not move.

"Not at the outset." She swallowed hard. "Later maybe when you've transfused a lot of blood, not right when we first get 'em usually." She glanced at Jake who had taken an interest in the Geiger counter.

Jake tapped on the sensor. "What did the portal monitor detect?"

"I'm not at liberty to discuss that in any depth." Atwood stepped back, apparently unaware of the response he'd flared in Tracy. "Gamma rays, I suspect."

Jake shook his head and fiddled with the controls on the sensor box. His shoulder twitched every second or third flip of the switch.

"An unshielded source," Tracy said, turning from the trauma record and confronting Atwood. "For gamma rays, you're talking about a source, not just some random contamination."

He shuffled on the tile and shrugged.

"Well, it's not here," Tracy said.

"We don't know." Atwood snatched the instrument from Jake. "Where's the body and his clothing ... did he have anything else with him when you found him?" He stood close to Jake. Another one of those alpha-male testosterone things.

Jake breathed out deeply but did not return the agent's stare.

Atwood studied Jake. "Right. We can—"

"The morgue is this way," Tracy said as she turned the corner out of the trauma bay. "You probably don't need Jake anymore, right?"

Atwood followed her into the gurney-lined hallway, popped a toothpick in his mouth, and made a sipping sound. "We'll need to hit the crime scene again first thing in the morning. I'm thinkin' we're gonna need both of you up there."

"What the hell for?" Jake took a step toward the agent. "I got a lot of work to do before that storm closes in."

"Hey, hang tight," Atwood said. "Let me check out the basement here and the stiff's clothes. Maybe we'll get lucky and this case will close itself."

The hairs on her neck bristled from the "stiff" comment. "Do you mean we might all have been exposed to an unshielded radiation source?" She swallowed, attempting to relieve the bitterness in her mouth.

Deep wrinkles creased Atwood's forehead. He said nothing.

"Let's get this done," Jake said and took Tracy's arm in his hand, gentle and supportive. Similar to the help she'd received from Marines in Helmand, climbing steep access paths or being assisted from shelter holes after mortar attacks. Except, this hand-up had a personal connection, a memory. An old fire rekindled in her chest, deep to her core. Tantalizing skin longing to be stroked and squeezed by his powerful hands, as it had been once before. Her heart beat accelerated.

She glanced expectantly at Jake. He snatched his hand away like fingers from a hot stove. A coy smile escaped the corner of her mouth. He felt it too.

Atwood leafed through the loose papers of the Kincaid file at the registration counter. "I thought you said labs were drawn?" He reshuffled a few sheets and turned several over as well.

"They're back," Tracy said. "I grabbed a copy just as we were leaving to meet the Sheriff. It's out in my overnight pack. We can get another copy." She asked the front desk clerk to call up the results and print them off before they returned from the morgue.

"They were pretty screwed up. I remember his platelet count being really low." Tracy pushed through a double door into a wide access hall. She stretched her neck and stifled a yawn. It had been a long day.

"From the resuscitation?" Atwood asked, his Dan Post cowboy boots echoed tap, tap down the hospital linoleum hallway.

"No ... not really." Tracy stopped before a windowless gray metal door and paused as she held the handle. "We drew blood right from the start as a baseline. Other than being acidotic everything should have been relatively normal. Stephen was a healthy young kid, at least he should have been."

She pulled open the door. The preservative and antiseptic smell of formaldehyde and bleach announced they had arrived in the morgue.

•

Jake stood just inside, unsure of the real and perceived dangers that may lurk in the repository for the dead. Across the room a glassed door, centered on a glass wall, led to a room with troughed metal tables and overhead operating lights. Two gray metal government-issue desks, with metal in and out boxes, stood loaded with charts. Next to each sat computer consoles, one of which showed the text of an apparent autopsy.

"What else was outside the normal ranges?" Atwood asked.

Tracy stopped before entering the autopsy room and with a twitch at the corner of her mouth considered Atwood. "I don't recall but he was obviously sick with something before he got to us and probably before he was shot."

Atwood swept the wand of the radiation detector about the office space. The lazy *click click* never changed and the needle stayed pegged at the lower end of the scale. He cautiously approached the door but was interrupted by a big-bosomed Hispanic lady in a white lab coat who stepped from behind a brushed-steel storage cabinet in the glass-enclosed room.

She pushed the door open, long bouncing brown hair with highlights framed a smile of straight white teeth. "Tracy, girl, I thought you'd had enough of this place earlier in the day." "Dr. Amelia Nuñez, Pathology" was embroidered in thick blue thread above the lapel pocket of her lab coat.

Tracy made introductions and explained their need to examine the body of Stephen Kincaid and his clothing.

Dr. Nuñez frowned. "I haven't started on the boy yet. Don't know if I will at all, actually. From what I heard, Sheriff Schaffer wanted the body sent to Rapid City for forensic testing." She eyed the Geiger counter in Atwood's hand. "What's that all about?"

Atwood gawked at Tracy. Right, like she was going to come up with some great cover story.

Tracy shrugged. "Hey, it's your rodeo, cowboy." She stood back and waved off Atwood.

Jaw clenched. Atwood studied Doctor Nuñez. "Homeland Security has interest in this case and we're trying to dot all the Is and cross the Ts before we close things out ... one of those Ts is to document any potential radiation or chemical-biological tie-ins."

Nuñez twisted pink latex gloves in her hands. She stared at Atwood and continued her frown. "Yeah right, what ya want, agent?"

"Just to look at the body and examine the clothes."

Nuñez eyed Jake. "The Sheriff okay with this, you think?"

"Yeah, we just came from the dispatch station," Jake said.

Nuñez pointed to shelves of gowns, gloves, and masks. She handed Jake a bottle of wintergreen off the desk. "You might like a little of this on your mask, Hon."

"Oh, I'm not going in," Jake said. A flush rose up his neck. He didn't care, there was no reason he needed to muck around with a dead Stephen Kincaid anymore, especially with the radiation contamination and all.

Nuñez nodded to the far side of the examination room. "Bin

eleven," she said.

The stench of death intensified as Tracy opened the glass door and a fresh gust of bleach, formaldehyde and rot invaded the office. Jake grabbed the wintergreen and rubbed several drops under his nose. He handed the bottle to Tracy, who doused her mask and passed it to Atwood.

Both took advantage of the gowns and gloves as well.

The Geiger counter continued to lazily click at a natural background radiation level. Atwood went straight to bin eleven and pulled out the body on wheeled tracks. He unzipped the white plastic bag and waved the detector probe over the naked corpse. No change. He slipped a camera from his shirt pocket and snapped a picture of the boy's face. Then, he stepped back and slowly moved his head from left to right. And finally, took a picture of the morgue, including Jake standing with the glass door ajar, which seemed to satisfy his discontent.

As he moved the Geiger counter close to the boy's feet, near a clear plastic bag of bloody clothing, the clicking increased in frequency.

Tracy stepped back as the agent studied the monitor.

"It is only trace levels of gamma rays," Atwood said. "Even so, this kid was definitely in contact with a source in the recent past ... What I don't know is did he wash these clothes since that time. If so the exposure could have been pretty high."

"Anything to worry about?" Tracy asked.

"Not as long as you don't eat his clothes." Atwood turned off the instrument. He unzipped the body bag further. "Kill shot, left chest. Someone knew what they were doing."

He zipped the bag closed walked to the sink and washed his hands.

"So, the Kincaid killing is connected to the radiation signature. But how?" Atwood asked as he intensely held Jake's gaze.

Acid in the pit of Jake's stomach tried to climb into his throat. He very much disliked this arrogant bastard. "Maybe you'll actually succeed in finding something out ... this time, Carl. And who the hell was shooting at us?"

He caught Tracy's amber eyes over the light blue mask. She radiated concern—for him it seemed.

Chapter 12

Patriot's Hospital Parking Lot

Carl Atwood had to meet the Homeland Security team at the Sheriff's office to arrange the morning sweep up Horse Thief Ridge. Packer's fan, Chad, would cover Tracy's morning shift in the ER and she'd already arranged Christmas off. She stood next to Jake's truck watching Jake shake his head. The pure, crisp freshness of new fallen snow surrounded them.

"I know what you're thinking," she said. The halo of light in the hospital parking lot did nothing to mute the icy cold that painfully numbed her earlobes. She once again pulled the sides of her Thinsulate stocking cap as far down as she could.

He brushed the accumulated snow off the driver's side door of the aged truck. "You might be able to get your Focus out to the ranch ... but I'll guarantee you, you'll never get back into town tomorrow afternoon."

She'd driven the Ford all the way from San Diego early in the fall, and sadly had not yet purchased snow-tires or chains. The weather report called for well over a foot of snow by evening. "So much for the beauty of a white Christmas." Tracy leaned into the snow-covered bed of Jake's truck to retrieve her backpack.

"Yeah, and another seven months of it." He slapped his gloves together. "I'll follow you to your apartment and drive you out to the ranch—"

"Tonight you mean?" Tracy brushed snow off her pack. "You're saying I should spend the night at the ranch?" Tightness gripped her chest.

"Well, yeah—you'd have to, with the storm and all." Jake twisted his unshaven chin in a cute embarrassed little twitch.

"Movin' pretty fast aren't you, Cowboy?" She put her hands on her hips and stared up into piercing blue eyes. Weathered creases shown at the edge of those eyes.

"Ten years is movin' fast?"

"Oh!" She laughed. "Still quick on your feet, I don't remember the scrambling quarterback being much interested in the skinny kid down the street."

"Hell, you were jail bait back then. Besides, you've got to remember you're talking to a guy whose female exposure in the past few years has been typically four-legged with as many teats." He winked. "Opening a truck door and tipping my hat takes concentration."

He was as adorable as ever. How did Natalie ever let him go? And what the hell happened with the Park Service? She studied the bald tires on her compact car. She might not even make it to her apartment. No kidding!

"Let's not talk anymore about teats, okay?" She left her bag in the truck bed and closed the tailgate. "You going to get me back to town in time for the Christmas pageant tomorrow night?"

"Are you serious?" He stared up into the sky, arms spread wide. "No one's gonna be drivin' around this town tomorrow night except someone in a sleigh with reindeer."

"We'll stop at the church on the way out and see if they've got any ideas yet." She scratched her scalp through the stocking cap and stared up into the falling snow. "Or a contingency plan."

"The old Lutheran Church?"

"Yeah—it's pretty much non-denominational now." Her cold insensitive fingers fumbled for the keys in her pocket. Gloves didn't help any.

"I haven't been in awhile."

"Since your dad died," she said it before she thought. Everyone had known he'd stopped going to church, it just wasn't talked about. A cold tingle ran down her spine, she actually shivered.

"Better get you out of the cold." He turned and walked around the truck.

That was stupid. She thought to say something else, but what?

Instead they each climbed into their vehicles and she tried the best she could to avoid spinning and sliding down side streets to her apartment. Should she ask him if he wanted to stay in town at her apartment tonight? No, that wouldn't work. He had cattle to take care of.

What should she take with her? She had flannel pajamas and Arizona State athletic sweats. She had frilly underwear she'd not worn in years. *Lord, Tracy, get a grip.*

•

Jake held back, giving Tracy and the Ford Focus plenty of maneuvering room. It was comical watching her ease the car around downhill corners, nearly sliding sideways in the process. She'd certainly gotten him sideways with the comment about his dad's death. It just didn't seem right. Why would God let a good man in the prime of his life be snatched away from his family? And just before Christmas. His dad had always dreamed of ranching and the trail he'd been cutting along his uncle's property would have allowed both of them to access Bureau of Land Management pasture to graze their cattle.

His dad didn't have any cattle at the time and had just made the down payment on a small ranch that cozied up to his uncle's. All lost within a year after the freak backhoe accident, a rollover, killed his father. His mother did get some of the money back, though with the double closing costs and the funeral, well, he'd been real lucky to get a scholarship otherwise college would've been out.

He chuckled. *Whoa!* At least she was getting the knack of it. Tracy pumped the brakes and eased her car shakily between a jeep and a king-cab pickup angling into an icy parking place.

He swallowed hard. What was going to happen at the ranchhouse tonight? What did she expect? His stomach knotted. He'd always figured on having a wife and kids some day, probably. But he'd never considered bringing a woman to the dilapidated structure before he'd had a chance to fix it up.

She was back down the steps in minutes, opened the truck door, and threw a black zippered travel bag on the seat between them. She smiled as she slid her hips up onto the seat.

"Do we have to go by the church?" he asked.

"Don't start." She pointed a finger at him.

"Yes, Mother." He pushed the clutch and shifted into reverse. His mother's finger-pointing had never worked. She'd been too soft on him after his dad's death. Jake, Catherine and their mother had all gone their own miserable ways after that terrible winter. It wasn't right, he knew that. At least his mother had reconciled with his sister. She'd have been around to help him as well if he'd just met her halfway.

Tracy sat quietly. He'd been insensitive, a common occurrence with Natalie—mutual barbs, many hurtful. Tracy refused to play that game. She was above that. He should be also.

"Sorry, I guess I need some remedial training in being civil ... especially with women."

"No, I opened a can of worms." She turned on the seat, facing him.

He concentrated on the slippery road and wall of snow that continued to fall. A lump tried to rise in his throat. He'd spoken some to his mother and Catherine about his dad's death but never with anyone else, not even with Natalie. Shoot he'd never considered talking to Natalie about it. "Mom and Catherine still go to church some."

"I've seen them a few times," Tracy said.

Jake checked the mirror, and finally glanced at Tracy. She wasn't staring at him any longer. "Parkin' out front gonna be okay?"

She smiled and nodded. "That'll be fine ... I'll just be a minute. Practice is probably over by now."

The Eastside Church had been renamed from Trinity Lutheran. The red brick building sported a fresh coat of white paint on the windows and a cross-topped spire typical of the early '60s when the church had been built. Flood lights gave the gold cross an unearthly glow that dragged Jake back to happier days—family days when life had seemed so simple and kindly.

At times like this Jake was almost inspired to think up a prayer. He didn't though. God was not real interested in Jake's life.

He studied the nativity scene out front of the chapel. There were more figures than he remembered. When he'd attended there had just been animals and shepherds, no wise men with colorful and varied hats. Where was the baby Jesus? He could clearly see the empty manger. Had someone taken the baby statue? Who would do that—an adolescent prank? He'd done his share, always in good fun. Should he say anything to Tracy? He didn't want to upset her or cause any delays getting back to the ranch.

She didn't notice, even though she walked right past the wooden structure with floodlights shining. Departing children waved at them as she climbed back into the truck, cold air spiraled into the cab along with a sprinkling of snow. She smiled brightly, her eyes reflecting the bright colors of the nativity scene.

"What'd Reverend Paul have to say?" Jake asked. He adjusted the heat vent toward Tracy.

"They won't make a decision until the morning." She held her gloved hands over the heating vent. "Sounds like they have no contingency … either it's a go or not. If not, it's next year."

"Right, we'll call. As long as the storm doesn't knock out the cell coverage."

As if by providence, Jake's cell phone rang the second he mentioned coverage. It was Catherine asking if he was still in town and did he intend to stop by and pick up Duke on his way to the ranch.

She also wanted a ride to the Sheriff's station. Sheriff Schaffer had asked her to have a look at the computer before he turned it over to the Feds.

♦

Jake didn't like it. He knew the crap that could rain down if you got on the wrong side of the Feds. He had worked hard at keeping a low profile for the past two years and certainly had never wanted to open his family to that level of scrutiny and persecution. And always popping up was Carl Atwood—there was something sinister about the guy. Jake could just not put it any other way.

"You don't look too happy about all this," Tracy said.

Jake caught himself staring at the road and chewing his lip. "I hope I'm not getting Cat in the cross-hairs of those fed bullies."

"Can you trust Sheriff Schaffer and his people to keep her out of it?"

"Honestly, I'm not sure any of us want to know what's on that computer." Jake glanced at Tracy. "I mean, someone killed Stephen and shot at us earlier … and now we're talking about nuclear contamination."

Tracy put her hand back on his arm. "If the Sheriff and you don't get a lead on what is happening here, the FBI and those other guys are going to bind it all up and seal it under a veil of national security."

Jake pulled behind his mother's Grand Cherokee. The sinking of his stomach fought against the burning in his scalp.

"If it's left to the Feds," Tracy said. "It will be just like in the Gulf. They'll only tell you what they want you to know, which is nothing or a cover story. Worse yet they may sweep it under the rug and you'll never know what happened to Stephen or even why there was a radiation signature near your ranch and cattle."

The front light to his mother's house came on and Catherine picked her way carefully down the stairs from the front porch as Duke did his best to knock her on her ass.

"If you can live with that." Tracy said. "Then tell Cat to go back in the house and we'll call the Sheriff and tell him we don't want to be involved … I don't know how well that is going to sit with Agent Atwood in the morning though."

Tracy put her backpack in her lap and slid next to Jake on the bench seat as Catherine opened the passenger door and allowed Duke to jump into the foot well on the passenger's side.

"Tracy meet Duke." Catherine laughed. "Sheriff said he'd give me a lift back afterward so you can get out to the ranch before too late."

Duke, tongue hanging out and tail wagging, gleamed at Tracy when she grabbed both his ears and scratching like a banshee put her nose next to his. "We've met," she said. "What a cute boy. Where's your daddy been hiding you?"

Jake couldn't keep the smile from creasing his mouth at the sight of the canine completely giving it over to a pretty girl. "Yeah, well, it seems ol' Duke and I have been pretty much on the road since yesterday morning … with all the happenings and whatnot."

"Are you going out to the ranch tonight?" Catherine asked Tracy, her eyes sparkling with the inferred connotation.

"Hang on there, Cat," Jake interjected. "This whole situation is getting worse not better."

"What do you mean?" Catherine's eyes opened wide. She glanced furtively at Tracy.

"I mean with the Sheriff, the FBI, Homeland Security and God only knows who else." Jake feathered the gas to keep the engine revved up. "Something is rotten with all this, Cat. And I can't tell you everything, but lately it seems whenever the Feds and especially Carl Atwood are around … I end up being the fall guy." He studied the falling snow through the driver's side window before picking his next words. "This could involve you as well—if you do this computer thing for Sheriff Schaffer."

Catherine unzipped her coat and sat back. She studied both Jake and Tracy's eyes for a hint of what was going on. "They can't fire me, Jake."

"I really don't know what they can or will do, Cat."

"You're not seriously suggesting that the Feds had anything to do with what happened to Stephen Kincaid … are you … I mean. Well I really don't know what I mean." Catherine shifted her gaze to Tracy when Jake refused to hold eye contact with her.

"Cat—" Tracy rested her hand on Jake's thigh. "We don't have a clue what Stephen was into or if he was just at the wrong place at the wrong time."

"At Jake's ranch?" Catherine asked.

"Exactly," Jake said. "And Carl Atwood is not about to let that connection rest. He'll push the issue to anyone who'll listen."

"This isn't getting us anywhere." Tracy stared at Jake beneath raised eyebrows. "You need a plan. You need to figure out what is going on and how to get the Feds off your back."

"And you need to know what Stephen was up to," Catherine said. "If anything."

Jake exhaled slowly through his nose and nodded. "Well, we didn't learn much at his parents' house—both the Sheriff and I think Clint Kincaid was holding something back."

"And what about the Koran?" Tracy asked. "I'd love to get a look at his emails and favorites list."

"All right, all right, but I'm not going to twist your arm, Cat," Jake said. "It's up to you."

"Jake, I think you either start fighting these people or hide with your tail between your legs like a dog."

Tracy scrunched her mouth at Catherine's rant.

"That's most of the problem," Jake pushed back. "I don't know who these people are … someone or some group in the federal government. But who I'm not sure."

"Why are they after you?" Tracy asked.

"I don't know." Jake shook his head in frustration. "Honestly, I don't even know if they are after me or if I'm just what they call 'collateral' damage."

"With your firing you mean?" Tracy asked.

Catherine nodded. "There was something odd with all that."

Duke tried to jump in between them on the bench seat and Catherine calmly patted him on the head. "It was like they just wanted you to go away ... and you did."

"It's that 'they' again." Jake once again revved the engine and tapped the clutch as the truck rocked a bit before sliding back into the icy snow covered road. "I guess it's time to start finding some answers ... hopefully it won't kill us."

Christmas lights blinked to life on the house across the street followed by a backlit nativity scene. The kneeling Virgin Mary stared at Jake.

Chapter 13

"Any luck?" Sheriff Schaffer leaned in through the lunchroom door. In the back of the station, the lunch room had been picked as the most out of the way location for a stealthy clandestine examination of Stephen Kincaid's laptop.

"No," Catherine said. "I've been through every personal date and name I can come up with and all the combinations. Of course if he reversed the letters and dates—like you should for a password—well, I can start on that but it may be till midnight just cycling through those variations."

Tracy shrugged her shoulders and fastened the top button on her sweater. The dry cold chilled her to the bone. It was probably economical to keep the Sheriff's Station at sixty-five degrees. But in the north facing back of the building, the frigid Dakota winter wormed its way through the cinder block walls and sucked the heat from your marrow it seemed.

Jake, foot propped on a metal and blue plastic dining chair, sipped his third cup of coffee, good luck getting to sleep tonight.

"What if Stephen was a serious Islam convert?" Tracy said.

The Sheriff scanned the nearly deserted Station.

"I mean maybe his password is from the Koran or in Arabic or Farsi … whatever."

Tracy typed in *Koran* and then *Islam*. Nothing.

"How about 'Allah Akbar' or 'God is great'?" Jake chimed in for the first time in nearly a half an hour.

Catherine pounded on the keyboard. "We're in!" she shouted.

"That was it."

Tracy blew out through pursed lips. "Really, 'Allah Akbar'. That's not reassuring news to me."

The Sheriff closed the door and pulled a chair behind Catherine. Jake leaned over Tracy who sat close to his sister. The linoleum and Formica-decorated room was quite as a tomb, except for the *tap, tap* of Catherine's fingers across the keys.

The next hour was enlightening. Stephen Kincaid was indeed an Islamic convert. Most of his email correspondence, though, with innocuous users such as Gbarbie5 and Go-muscle-car, seemed cryptic and suspicious when viewed sequentially and in total.

Sheriff Schaffer directed examination of several saved threads. "Seems to be a lot of traffic about his visit back home, with a few references to people that are probably not family members."

Catherine deftly pounded out instructions and clicked about the web pages sending various messages to a zip drive she'd brought with her.

Jake had waited patiently but twice had started pacing the room while Catherine followed the Sheriff's instructions. Finally he pushed up between Catherine and the Sheriff. "You guys ready to look at his favorites site?"

The Sheriff nodded to Catherine and slid to the left. Jake grabbed the nearest chair and swung it around backward, sitting horseback style, hands folded on the chair back.

Catherine backed out of two or three windows and then hit the heart-shaped icon. South Dakota and Wyoming sites for music festivals along with several sites on dating filled the screen.

"Oh crap!" the Sheriff said.

"No, wait." Catherine used the mouse to advance down a long list of favorites. "Those are probably from when he was here in Palmer ... maybe even from when he was in high school." The screen continued to scroll and finally they reached the bottom.

"Right," Tracy said pointing at the bottom half dozen site names. "These are the ones he's been on recently."

Silently all four of them read the bottom sites. Belatedly a fan kicked on and blew warm air from a vent near their feet. Tracy inched to the right placing her feet directly on the vent. *Thank God!* She flexed her numb, aching toes as sensation painfully returned. Her mind, which had been on autopilot through most of search, now reacted like it had been infused with a pot of coffee.

"What the hell!" Sheriff Schaffer removed his reading glasses and leaned close to the screen. "Can you save that?" he asked Catherine.

"I don't know. But we can take a picture of it with my cell phone and download it wherever you want."

"Don't send it over the web," Jake said. "Once it gets into the cloud, it's anyone's baby."

Tracy nodded to the Sheriff's breast pocket as Catherine snapped pictures with her iPhone. "Maybe it's time to go old-school."

The Sheriff frowned.

"Copy them down in your notebook," she said.

Interspersed among several Islamic sites were three particularly disconcerting notations. The last one was the National Institute of Health site on Acute Radiation Sickness. Three lines above that was an unclassified Homeland Security summary of radio-isotope detection devices. But the one that held Tracy's attention was halfway up the page and included Russian Cyrillic nomenclature and the number 115.

"Sheriff Schaffer," echoed down the hallway. Carl Atwood!

"Shut it down," he said to Catherine and simultaneously hit the light switch. Dull red emergency lighting shown from across the lunch room. He pointed to the rear exit and whispered. "I'll meet you out back ... five minutes."

Tracy was two steps behind Catherine and Jake right behind her. The door opened quietly.

"Down here." The Sheriff pushed through the double door.

Atwood could be heard toward the front of the station moving back toward them. "Is Jake Moran here?" he asked.

The Sheriff reacted quickly knowing that Jake's truck was still out front with his dog. "Just finished reviewing his statement on the killing ... I think he's around here somewhere."

Jake ushered the women out the back door into the glare of a street light reflecting off a deluge of large snowflakes. He turned and walked around the corner of the lunch room into the main hallway. Tracy kept the door ajar, her heart racing.

"What'ya need, Carl?" muffled some as he turned the corner.

Gently Tracy eased the door shut. It locked with a faint click.

Icy cold seemed to invade her from every direction. Catherine, eyebrows raised, said nothing.

"That's the Sheriff's truck," Tracy said pointing to a covered and lighted bay. "Probably too much to ask that it be unlocked."

Catherine shivered and pulled a reindeer decorated scarf tightly around her neck. "Just another night in Paradise."

•

"I don't trust him." Atwood stopped just short of poking the Sheriff in the chest with his index finger. "He's a civilian with a questionable past, let me remind you."

He whispered but not quietly enough.

Jake stepped out of the shadowed hallway into the Station's foyer. "No date tonight, Carl?" Jake bit down as soon as he'd said it. There was nothing to be gained by aggravating this jackass.

Atwood turned, a crooked smile on his lips. "Jake … retirement on the ranch getting boring?"

"Wouldn't I like that." Jake patted the Sheriff on the back. "I'll check with you again when I get back in town day-after-tomorrow. Okay, Sheriff?"

"That'll be fine. You folks be careful tomorrow."

"Expect me early, Ranger." Atwood stepped eye-to-eye, invading Jake's personal space. "This damn storm is closin' in fast."

Swallowing hard, Jake stepped past the agent. "I'll leave the light on, case you get out before sunup. You might drive right past the place in the blowin' snow otherwise." He waved at the portly dispatcher as he pushed open the front door.

Atwood said something to the Sheriff about a possible meeting in the morning at the Travel Lodge up the road if snow conditions didn't worsen. The blowing wind sent the rest of his comments somewhere off to Iowa, Jake guessed.

In addition to at least another three inches of snow, the wind had pushed a drift nearly up to the truck's door. Duke grudgingly gave up the warm, driver's seat where he'd apparently settled in for the night. He did thump his tail respectfully—happy to see his master—or at least the guy that fed him every day.

Through the glass door Sheriff Schaffer did an admirable job of playing at political correctness with the jerk FBI agent. The frigid steering wheel of the old Ford had not had the benefit of Duke's warm body. Jake slipped on gloves as he surveyed the parking lot. Around the west side of the building, several trailers and a tracked snow vehicle sat off the pavement in the dark. Jake shifted into four wheel low and let the truck idle around the building while the Sheriff occupied Atwood.

On the north side of the last trailer he backed his pickup nearly up against the hillside, turned off his lights and killed the engine. Tracy and Catherine stood blowing in their hands near the Sheriff's truck.

Within five minutes the black FBI Tahoe accelerated out the front of the parking lot and up the hill to the west, toward the Travel Lodge Motel. Light shown from the back door of the Sheriff's station and Schaffer ambled across into the covered parking to his vehicle and the girls. The heater had started to work when Jake pulled up next to the three. Window down and defroster on maximum he listened.

"Okay." Catherine gestured with her cell phone. "I'll copy down Stephen's web sites. It would be best if you stopped by the Mountain Rose to pick them up though."

"What about the zip drive?" Tracy handed it to Catherine.

"Oh Lord." Catherine rolled her eyes. "I completely forgot about it while I was shutting the laptop down."

Jake's stomach twisted into a knot. "Hey, relax it's okay." He willed the tightness out of his neck. "Thanks Tracy. Look, we've all got to watch each other's back. Double and triple check everything—we can't afford any slipups. They're watching everything we do."

"Cat, I'd just give the zip to the Sheriff," Tracy said. "You certainly can't send any of it over the internet and even making a copy can probably be detected on whatever device you use."

"What about Stephen's contacts?" Jake asked. "Can we somehow get a lead on their internet activities?"

Catherine glanced at the Sheriff. "I would think that would take a warrant or something to access their data at Gmail or wherever."

"Yeah," the Sheriff said. "I appreciate what you've all done. And I'll keep it under my hat but the rest of that stuff is gonna have to be done by the FBI and Homeland Security."

"So what do you make of his Islamic contacts and the radiation websites?" Jake asked.

The Sheriff scrunched his mouth and glanced around the group.

His gaze settled on Catherine. "I think we've gone as far as we can with this tonight." He fixed Jake's stare and nearly imperceptibly shook his head. The intent was clear. He did not want drones or radiation detection discussed in front of Cat.

"Kinda blows the murder investigation wide open," Tracy said.

To no one in particular, the Sheriff mumbled. "Yeah, kinda."

Tracy took the zip drive from Catherine's hand, gave it to the Sheriff, hugged Catherine and walked around the front of the pickup into the falling snow of the headlights. "Mums the word, girlfriend," she said to Catherine while putting a finger over her lips. "You about ready, Cowboy?" She kicked the snow off her boots as she climbed in next to Duke.

Tracy sat quietly warming her hands on the hot air from the console heater as Jake settled the rattling work truck into a reasonable four-wheel pace east, out of town.

Other than dinner the previous night at the Mountain Rose, their reintroduction had been a catastrophe. CPR on a murder victim shot at on Horse Thief Ridge, and now risking federal obstruction of justice charges. He'd be lucky if, at her first real opportunity, she didn't run away waving her arms and screaming.

Warmed up, she finally leaned back against the passenger's door fiddling with a tassel on the end of her scarf. She stared at Jake and the edges of her mouth softened into a smile. "On the way to the ranch you want to tell me what happened with the Park Service? No one seems to want to say much about it."

Jake broke the stare, a tightness gripping his chest. He blew out slowly against the already fogged windshield. Pushed the heater knob to defrost and swallowed hard. "I think people are more concerned about not spreading rumors about Natalie than they're really thinking much about the hikers' incident."

From the floor board below Tracy, Duke nudged Jake's leg and whined halfheartedly.

"Hikers?"

"Yeah." He pulled the hat off and set it between them on top of her backpack. "Well, probably more accurately, the climbers' investigation."

He shifted and eased the clutch gently, coaxing power carefully to the four wheels. Snow crunched as the rusted farm truck plotted warily toward the ranch.

"The one where Bret Peterson was killed?" Tracy's hand edged behind Duke's ear and worked the loose skin in a circular motion. Duke's tongue lolled to the left as love and devotion pooled deep in the canine's eyes

Jake nodded. No one had cared much to hear his side of the story since his dismissal from the Park Service. They probably all thought he was in the wrong and had screwed up somehow. "It was Peterson's first year up here in the mountains … Just up from San Antonio." Acid burned in Jake's stomach. "A good guy, but really wet behind the ears when it came to the mountains and ice … I never understood why the Service transferred him up in the first place."

"He fell during a rescue. Is that right?"

He could feel her gaze searching every crevice in his face. He trembled. Maybe she wouldn't notice. "It was … It was a search and rescue for three lost hikers." His head shook, breathing deepened. "Supposed to be hikers anyway."

Tracy reached over to his hand just as he down-shifted. Their fingers interlaced. Hers felt cold, soft, and delicate. "It can wait, Jake." Her voice sweet, yet mature. A voice that had soothed suffering soldiers in far-away war zones. The ache in his chest eased. "Let's get a warm fire going and try to get some sleep before they start beating down the doors in the morning."

Duke's eyes closed again, lazily, when Tracy once again resumed her attack on the redundant skin on his neck and behind his ears.

Jake let the drag of the engine slow the truck as they eased around an indistinct curve. He didn't want to end up stuck in a ditch for the night. Probably best to concentrate on one problem at a time.

Tracy swung out of the truck almost before he'd stopped at the ranch gate. "Got it," she said, wrapping a gold-accented scarf high around her neck.

The amber in her eyes picked the mystic gold out of the scarf, mesmerizing. Like a beautiful snow maiden, skipping temptingly about a white winter wonderland.

Chapter 14

Moran Ranch House

Tracy fingered the Christmas dish towel hanging on the ancient gas stove. The scene depicted the Star of Bethlehem and shepherds in a field tending sheep. Thread-worn, it had seen better days. The Spartan yet clean kitchen was much as she'd remembered from her brief stop the previous day, but she hadn't noticed the meager attempt at holiday decorating. Along with the towel a small robed Santa, holding a scepter, sat atop the lone sideboard.

Stomping on the porch signaled Jake's return from the barn.

"How're the cattle?" she asked as he settled a huge snow shovel against the side of the house and closed the sturdy door. She imagined a timber being wedged behind the door to protect early settlers from marauders.

"Fine … hopefully I put up enough hay to get through the winter." He shrugged out of a fleece-lined, denim jacket and hung it on a worn bent horseshoe next to the door.

"Think we'll need that shovel to get out in the morning? Are we expecting that much snow?" Tracy hugged her fleece vest against her chest as flakes of snow drifted off Jake's hat and coat onto a stained throw rug.

Duke shook once at the door and eased over to a worn rag rug across from the fireplace.

Jake removed his boots and placed them strategically below the coat. Talk about OCD.

"It's happened before. Less now with the weather scans and all. Still, sometimes those November snows will creep up on you through the night." Gloves dropped next to the boots. "We can heat that chow from the hospital in the microwave." He pointed to the only new-appearing appliance in the kitchen.

"Your stomach recovered enough from your trip to the morgue for that?" Tracy stepped toward the ash-filled fireplace.

Jake rubbed his hands. "Sure. It wasn't that bad." A feeble smirk edged the side of his mouth. "I'll get a fire going if you can do the domestic chores?"

"Really, you're gonna let me take over your kitchen that easily?" He just scowled at her.

Tracy found a mismatch of dinnerware in the cupboards and transferred spaghetti and string beans onto two plates, one with Christmas decorations and another with a cowboy roping a steer. Jake made short work of starting a fire with a pile of kindling and split logs.

Duke's dinner from a yellow Purina bag was unceremoniously deposited in a quart-sized, blue bowl that looked like it was from the depression.

Paper towels served as napkins and she gave up on any place mats or table cloth after two trips around all the kitchen cabinets.

Jake sat on one of the three matching chairs at the table after filling two glasses with water from the tap and a second, matching depression-era bowl of water for Duke. "I've got some beer if you'd prefer?"

"I'll split one with you. You have to know though, I'm kinda a lightweight when it comes to alcohol." Tracy didn't want to dull her senses but her mouth moistened at the thought of washing the spaghetti down with a sweet ale.

Jake grabbed a couple of mason jars off a shelf and popped the lid off a Coors from the refrigerator. As he poured amazingly equal portions into the jars, Tracy presented him the plates. He chose the steer roper.

"Not in the Christmas spirit?"

He nodded toward the robed St. Nicholas. "Catherine and Mom were supposed to stop by Christmas Day … doubt they'll make it now."

Tracy wiped her hands on the faded Christmas hand towel and spread it flat on the oak table. "Yeah, you went all out. When do you put up the Christmas tree?"

"Attacked in my own home by the Ghost of Christmas Past."

Jake opened an ancient bread box sitting next to the Santa on the sideboard. "Bread, O specter of the night?"

The dinner conversation mellowed to discussions of high school classmates and where they had ended up. More lived in the area than Tracy would have expected. Natalie, was long gone to Minneapolis soon after her and Jake's falling out, a regional buyer for Penneys.

•

The fire quickly took the chill out of the small ranch house. Jake felt a twinge in his lower abdomen when Tracy stripped off her fleece vest and draped it over his coat on the hook next to the door. An invasion of his personal space? Still, it was an intimacy that he found not uncomfortable. In fact, the denim jacket and Indian-pattern fleece appeared very natural together.

He stood, back to the fireplace, letting the flames seep into his legs and back. "It'll be warmest up in the bedroom … I'll sleep down here on the sofa."

"I can't take your bed!" Tracy eased near the fire as well.

The redness on her nose had faded and her soft velvet complex-ion reminded him of the stark contrast between men and women's skin. He fought the urge to touch her face, remembered the soft-ness of her lips when she'd kissed him a decade ago. He swallowed hard. "Don't be crazy. I'll be down here for when the posse arrives."

She stepped forward and took his hands in hers. His chest tight-ened, heart beating in his neck. "Well, okay. As dead tired as I am, I'm not going to argue with you." Her tongue wetted her lips. "You sleep good." She whispered in a throaty voice, stood on tiptoes and kissed him sweetly on the cheek.

Her tantalizing scent assaulted him as the gentlest, most pleas-ant kiss he'd ever received sent tingling sensations streaking to the center of his brain. He held his breath.

The smell of burning oak drifted between them as she slid away. He breathed deeply.

She smiled at him, the genuine and innocent smile he'd seen years earlier. "If you need to come up and get some blankets or a pillow just give me a minute to get changed." She stooped and retrieved her overnight bag.

His heartbeat slowed. "Make yourself at home. Just push my stuff to the side of the counter if you need room."

She climbed the narrow staircase with feline grace, seeming as natural an extension of the house as the ancient stove and fireplace. Her petite frame actually fit the restricted stairs better than his. He sighed deep and turned to the fire, the warm glow in his chest more than just heat from the burning embers.

•

Tracy played her hand across the cotton-blend bedspread in the small upstairs bedroom, brown and tan geometric shapes—a man's room. The storm rattled the wood-frame windows mercilessly. One more day until Christmas. She had groceries to buy and still had to decorate for the pageant. It wasn't going to all get done. She knew that. *Crap!* She might not even get back into Palmer before Christmas.

And what the hell was going on with radiation signatures north of Jake's ranch and on Stephen Kincaid's clothing? Carl Atwood was soft-playing it but his timetable for investigation suggested otherwise.

Tracy reflected on the testosterone-induced confrontation between Atwood and Jake. These two had a history. Best to keep them wide apart if at all possible. She knew Jake and she trusted him. Atwood was another story.

"You decent?" echoed up the stairs.

"As good as I'm going to be. Come on up."

Jake's six-foot-plus frame more than filled the old stairwell as he ducked his head into the bedroom. "They sure didn't build these houses for football players, did they?"

Tracy sat cross-legged on the full-sized bed in sweat pants and an Arizona State jersey. Braless, she knew the jersey left little to the imagination. His look lingered briefly, like most men's.

Standing in the room his head nearly brushed the support beams. "My plan is to build a master bedroom off the side of the living room ... with a fourteen-foot ceiling."

"That would make it a great bachelor pad." She laughed.

"Yeah, just need a Jacuzzi tub and a heart-shaped bed."

"Wow, you are such a romantic." She threw a pillow in his direction, which he caught and whipped back at her, chuckling.

"I'll just be a minute." He grabbed a blanket from the bottom drawer of a dresser and one of the pillows from the bed, tossed them down the stairs, and ducked into the hall bathroom.

Water ran, soap squished, and a toothbrush was deposited in a glass cup. Creeping quietly, she approached his bent-over profile from the back as he wrung water from a floral patterned wash-cloth.

Without thinking, she found herself leaning against him, spooning his naked torso. His muscles tensed, the dribble of water into the sink stopped. He didn't move. She lay her cheek against his broad shoulders and rubbed her hand purposefully across his rippled abdomen. Her breasts molded naturally against his lower back and the taut muscles of his buttocks, confined by his pants, nestled her stomach.

"It's a wonderful old homestead," she said.

He folded the cloth and placed it on the edge of the sink. "You've got me at a disadvantage." He stared alluringly at her reflection in the mirror.

"Just where I want you." She moved her hands playfully up and stroked his chest as she kissed his back.

He turned, a bulge evident in his pants. "It needs some work," he said, shifting awkwardly.

"Don't we all?"

"I was talking about the house," he murmured brushing a loose strand of hair behind her ear. Boldly he stepped into her. The full-ness of his manhood pressed into her abdomen.

She melted like the liquid wax of a candle spilling from a flame. He tilted her head up to meet hungry lips that sweetly enveloped her mouth—tasting, probing. The thin fabric of her jersey did nothing to stem the fire between them.

He pulled her head to his chest, chin resting in her hair. "That was nice," he whispered.

She pulled back and smiled brightly into his piercing eyes. "The best." She dropped her eyes to his bare chest.

He stepped back hands on her shoulders. "Yes ... I think it was." He glanced over her shoulder to the bed, sighed. "I think I would ask for a rain-check on this if you don't mind ... when we've got the time to explore it all properly."

"Right." She plopped back on the bed as his love-starved eyes continued to examine her.

Hand-massaging his neck, his head shook ever-so-slightly. "I was right to stop ten years ago you know."

"You are such a cowboy, Jake Moran." Tracy laughed. "That rain check is going to be due and payable in the not to distance future. Trust me."

"I'm good to my word." Jake crossed his heart. "We just need some sleep so we can keep our wits about us tomorrow."

"Any idea what is going on with this radiation stuff and the Kincaid kid? Everything seems to be connected."

"What could it be? Theft of radioactive isotopes … or terrorism in South Dakota?" Jake stepped into the bedroom and put a foot up on the bed. "What could possibly be around Palmer for hijacking or anything?"

"They sure were down here fast," Tracy said.

"Yeah, and you can bet Carl Atwood is only going to tell us what he needs us to know and nothing more." He sighed through clenched teeth.

"You and Carl friends in the past?"

"Not exactly." He chortled. "More like mutual interests … apparently conflicting mutual interests." He exhaled, holding his jaw fixed. "A quilt my mother gave me last Christmas is in the top of the closet if you need it. Sorry if it smells like mothballs." He hesitated by the door, glanced back at Tracy. "Thanks for helping out today, and with Cat." He leaned over and delicately kissed her cheek. Before he could move she turned her head and lightly nibbled the corner of his mouth.

"Good night, Cowboy."

He stood over her, and for a moment, she didn't know what he was going to do. Then he turned, put a hand on the ceiling, and eased his way down to the main floor. Hopefully thinking of that night ten years ago in the hayloft.

Chapter 15

Moran Ranch

She awoke to barking and then pounding on the front door, wishing she'd brought her rifle inside with her. The LED display next to Jake's bed read 2:43 AM. Jake stood next to the door as she eased down the stairwell in her wool socks.

"Who is it?" Jake asked through the heavy timbers.

With the barking, she didn't hear the response but Jake must have because he unhinged the lock and opened the door. Cool air billowed up the stairs as a flurry of snow blew into Jake's face. Carl Atwood, complete in L. L. Bean jacket and hunting cap, squeezed through the door, stomping snow from his boots.

"What are you doing here?" Jake asked as he turned on a lamp by the door.

Tracy eased herself down to the foyer careful not to step on any of the melting snow.

Atwood brushed snow off his cap and tossed it on the end table with the lamp. Unzipping his coat he scoffed at the old ranch house. "Thought you'd have more room out here than this." He shrugged out of the snow-covered coat and flipped it onto the kitchen table.

"Carl, it's nearly three o'clock in the morning." Jake stifled a yawn, picked up a metal iron and poked at the struggling embers in the fireplace.

Tracy stirred the fire and tossed two pieces of split wood on a small flame. Duke backed onto his rug without taking his eyes off Atwood.

"Snowin' like hell." Atwood grimaced at the empty coffee pot in the kitchen. "Cozy though, I guess … in a retro sort of way." He pulled the notebook out of his shirt pocket and flopped onto one of the kitchen chairs. "After reviewing the radiation readings and case notes on the Kincaid kid with the Homeland guy, I figured I better get my ass out here before another foot of snow settles in." He glanced up the stairwell and at the blanket and pillow on the sofa. "When was this place built?" He scoffed.

"Mid 1800s," Jake answered.

Tracy picked Atwood's jacket off the table and hung it over the horseshoe hook. His hat she placed on top. He didn't seem to notice, or assumed it was the woman-of-the-house's duties.

Jake rubbed a hand through his disheveled hair. "I wish you'd have called first—"

"Yeah, sorry to disturb you and the little lady." Atwood's gaze lingered on Tracy's chest.

For a smartly-dressed guy he sure had a crude side. She'd known the type—sailors with a girl in every port. This guy was a cowpoke with a punch in every trail town. His proclivity for infidelity clear. Tracy was not going to be his next punch. She wondered how many other trusts this arrogant bastard might betray.

She held his stare, once it rose to her face. "Looks like the inn is full, Joseph. Maybe the innkeeper has a manger out in the stable you could crawl into."

"Whoa, filly." The agent held his hands in the air. "I meant no ill intent. I mean, we're all adults here, right."

"Mostly," Tracy said.

Jake put his hands on each of their shoulders. "I shouldn't have to say this but chill, you two." He eased Tracy to the sofa and with hands on his hips faced Atwood. "As you can see the ol' homestead was not intended as a Bed-n-Breakfast."

The fireplace had once again sprung to life, dancing flames and a homey crackle. Jake did a double-take of the sofa, fireplace, and front door. "I don't have any more blankets or mattresses. You can sleep with some of the coats in front of the fireplace. I can move the coffee table back by the door."

Atwood rubbed his mouth and two-day growth of beard, glanced at Duke and then up the stairs. "Who's sleeping upstairs?"

"I am," Tracy said.

Atwood glanced from the sofa to Tracy. "Double bed?"

Tracy laughed. "In your dreams, Special Agent."

Jake made a throaty sound and shook his head.

"Hey, I'd keep my pants on … it's bad-ass cold as it is."

"Carl, this lady is a guest in my home." Jake picked the blanket and pillow off the sofa. "So let's knock off the greasy Don Juan crap." He threw the pillow on the floor. "I'll take the floor, you can have the sofa." He eyeballed Tracy, brows knitted and a grimace on the edge of his lips. "Did you end up using the quilt?"

She exhaled deeply. "It was still pretty cold."

Jake threw his hands up and climbed the stairs. "Maybe I've got another pillow or sheets in storage upstairs … I don't know." He disappeared into the darkness of the upstairs.

Tracy used the main floor half-bath and paused to put Chapstick on in the mirror as Jake rustle about above her. The door creaked and a hand settled on her hip.

"I always wonder what it would be like to corner a Wildcat," Carl Atwood's throaty baroque whispered near her ear.

"That's University of Arizona." Tracy turned and assessed the dancing eyes of the federal agent. "Arizona State is the Sun Devils. Careful what you wish for." She slid by him through the door, making more body contact than she'd have preferred, and slipped quickly up the stairs.

Jake had the light on in the extra room and turned with a shrug. "Great." He punched the light out and brushed a hand across her back. "Get some rest. See you in the morning."

She twisted into Jake's open shirt and bare abdomen. He pulled her up on her tiptoes, his steel-grey eyes tearing into her, the cloth between their chests dissolving. Soft lips brushed her cheek and then settled briefly on her quivering lips.

"Sleep tight," he whispered in her ear.

•

The night was a triple torture. Try as he might, Jake could not get Tracy Aspen out of his mind, or the arrogance of Atwood. The cold hardwood floors attacked the muscles of his back and deep into his spine with a vengeance. Finally, Carl Atwood snored, not loud but he did snore. Jake got up twice to put more of the dry wood on the fire, which burned too quickly. Even with his and Tracy's coats he repeatedly awoke, the chill from the floor seeping into his bones and joints.

Tomorrow would be miserable—and he would have no chance to fix the east fence line before the snows made the pasture impassable for the winter. Another of several critical tasks for the spring, before he let cattle into the pastures.

The crackle of the fire awoke him. No, the fire was nearly out again. He rolled to his side and noticed a shadowy silhouette move across the room. Atwood snored rhythmically with each breath. Tracy? What was she up to? He stretched his cold stiff leg and raised up on an elbow. She slid next to him, crouching close.

"What is it?" he whispered.

She placed a cool finger against his lips and blew a warm, "Shhh," in his ear.

He barely made out a crooking of her finger as she glided back to the stairwell. Duke's tail thumped rhythmically on the wood floor. Jake followed Tracy to the base of the stairs.

She leaned in close the scent of lilacs teased him to aroused awareness. With warm breath she whispered, "Come upstairs. It's freezing down here." A soft delicate hand took his and led him silently up the stairs.

She climbed into the bed and pulled the pile of quilt and blankets over herself. Reaching across the bed, she drew back the covers on his side. He slid onto a warm mattress and was instantly covered by blankets alive with Tracy's heady, feminine fragrance, obviously the side she'd been sleeping on. Welcoming wool socks scissored around his feet.

"You're like an icicle."

He bunched up his familiar pillow only to gather a handful of hair against his face as well. A fresh simplicity seized his attention. "What a nice scent," he whispered.

"It's Wen, green tea and herbs." She breathed lightly against his face.

"Hmm, I think I like it."

"You might just find there's a lot of things you like about me."

He rolled toward her, feeling the smooth roundness of her shapely hip against his loins. "I like your rifle." He murmured. "And I like you with a little more meat on your bones."

She turned to him. The softness of her abdomen enveloping his manhood as he struggled for control—and failed. Lips caressed his nose as delicately as a butterfly. "Do you always welcome girls to your house with talk of bones and erupting implements?"

"Only the fiery ones on the verge of a warpath."

"Do you see a lot of that around here … women on the warpath?"

"You're the first … woman, that is." Jake put his hand on her shoulder and lowered his mouth to her shadowed face. Eyelids faintly brushed his cheek as he nibbled his way to her subtle vibrating mouth. His lower lip was delightfully assaulted in a sweet attack of rosebuds and nectar.

Tracy moaned as she shifted to his ear whispering, "I've wondered for ten years what that lip tasted like."

"There are things I've wondered about for ten years also," Jake said. He breathed in the earthy wholeness of this winter nymph. "As it turns out, they were worth wondering about."

She rolled and pulled his arm around her, nestled firmly against his erect manhood, and sighed contentedly. "Good night, Jake."

Chapter 16

Mount Rushmore, Keystone, South Dakota

The first rays of sunshine crept across the alabaster faces of the American presidents, only to be extinguished by dark clouds that swirled over the crest above. Snow came intermittently. The sixteen inches of new snow had closed the roads into the national monument the previous night. It didn't matter though, Amir had seen the lights of snowplows since early morning. The Beacon of American capitalism would be open to traffic by the 27th of December. The meeting would go on.

His Toronto contact, Rashid, who wore robes trimmed in gold and jeweled rings on his fingers, had left a cryptic clean-cell text late last night. "Not to worry." Though new to the group, Amir was aware of their great and lucrative success delivering heroin to the weak-willed Americans. Now it was time to deliver to these dogs the flaming wrath of Allah.

Amir adjusted the high-power telescope by touch in the darkened hotel room. Curtains pulled nearly closed allowed in little light and absolutely no observation from outside. Truly, the President's View Hotel yielded a clear, though distant, panorama of Mount Rushmore.

Snow entirely covered the summit above the stone edifices. And throughout the night and early morning, Amir had seen no activity on or above the monument.

All was going as planned—he would do Allah's bidding again today. If the troublemakers tried to interfere he would be the fiery sword of Mohammad that would strike them down. It had surprised him to see a woman lead the farmer and local authorities up to the mountain overlook. He had not killed many women, maybe none. He'd shot women, but was not actually sure if any of them had died. In fact, he was unsure of many of his kills, but not Stephen Kincaid. He would kill the woman if necessary.

Amir did not like South Dakota. There were no criers or minarets to call for prayer. When circumstances allowed, at daily worship times, he would bow to the east and repeat the Islamic creed, or other holy writings. Sadly though, here in the belly of the infidels, caution must be taken. Danger and discovery lingered in the most unsuspected places.

The night before, as wind and snow howled, he'd sat near the fireplace in the hotel lobby and remembered the embrace of his wife, Haifa, on cold Toronto nights. He dreamed and prayed for the swift delivery of his mission and his safe reunion with his family, and eventually their return in honor to Persia.

•

Tracy threw the quilt over the shivering Carl Atwood. Bacon sizzled in a frying pan and coffee lazily percolated from the old school coffee pot. Through the frost-covered front window the occasional ray of sun would reflect off snow high on Horse Thief Ridge. No sustained daylight had yet to breech the impressive rock ledges to the east of the Lazy T.

Even the dull pounding of Jake in the shower had failed to awaken the federal agent. It couldn't be a good quality to sleep so soundly when in the field, on a mission. Tracy poured two cups of coffee as Jake eased down the stairs, clean shaven—hair still wet from the shower.

"Did you leave any hot water?" she asked.

"What! The warrior goddess needs warm water?" Jake snapped at her with a wet towel.

"You're on egg duty," she said, pointing a dangerous spatula in his direction. "I'll take 'em anyway you wanna fix them." She tweaked Atwood on the nose with the spatula, which brought minimal response. "Sleeping beauty probably needs a kiss from a frog to get him going this morning."

Jake pushed the fireplace log around a bit but did not add any more wood. "We should be out the door in less than an hour. I've got some snowshoes in the shed I'll throw in the back of the truck."

"I'll be ready with bells on," Tracy said as she pulled her jersey over her head on the way up the stairs. "Keep Buck-a-roo Bob downstairs till I'm out of the shower, okay?"

"Roger that," Jake said.

•

He'd awakened to the crackle and salty-sweet smell of bacon—the covers where flipped back on Tracy's side of the bed—pleasingly, her flowery fragrance lingered on the pillow and sheets. What would it be like to wake up next to her on a lazy winter morning with nothing to do but lay naked in each other's arms? Mornings with Natalie had always started with orders from Natalie. At first he'd liked pleasing her. Eventually it became apparent that he could never do enough. Leaving had been the best thing she'd ever done for him and that didn't say a lot.

Now standing over the stove, spatula in hand, Jake listened to the snoring Atwood. He didn't have to stretch his imagination much about Tracy's "Buck-a-roo Bob" comment. It occurred to Jake that whenever the FBI agent was around bad things happened.

Jake scrambled the eggs he had left in the refrigerator and threw in a few slices of cheese and dollop of milk to create a soft scramble his mother had been famous for.

The Star Spangled Banner chiming from Atwood's iPhone successfully roused the lead agent. "Talk to me," he said to the caller. "I don't give a damn if it is Christmas Eve—get me a warrant on the dad's ranch. We'll be at the site within the hour." Atwood listened for a couple of minutes, nodding. "Right." He rubbed his eyes, and belched.

"Help yourself to breakfast and coffee," Jake said. He grabbed two pieces of toast and slapped bacon and eggs in between. "I'm gonna make sure we can get out to the barn and then put some chains on the truck."

"Four wheel not good enough?" Atwood asked as he punched at the iPhone touch screen.

"Usually it is. I just want to make sure we can keep moving if we need to." Jake pulled Atwood's coat off the wall hook and slipped an arm into his. "We could end up spending the next week pulling trucks out of that field with my tractor if we're not careful."

Atwood nodded. "Homeland thinks they can fly a chopper up to your north pasture if the weather breaks for awhile."

"Yeah, they probably can. Lots of places to land, if we give them a little direction … and if the weather holds." Jake zipped the coat and slipped his hat on. "That's a big 'if' this time of the year though."

"The pretty lady gonna be ready to go?"

Jake hesitated before opening the door. "Are you sure you need her up there today?"

"Sheriff says she knows the area best … just in case we need to go up."

"You'd have to be crazy to try and climb up that cliff face in this weather. What are you guys really after … and who was shooting at us yesterday?"

"Need to know, Jakie-boy, need to know." Atwood scraped most of the eggs on a plate and grabbed a handful of bacon. "I'll tell you though. We've ID'd some pretty creepy people out there. They better not be treading on my territory."

"Right." Jake pulled open the door and pushed through a foot or so of snow. Most of the drifts had piled up on the other side of the house. Since Atwood was in line for chief of the South Dakota FBI, somewhere a "jackass quotient" existed in order to qualify for such positions. Thankfully, Tracy appeared to have correctly sized up the mid-life-crisis divorcee. And Atwood was hiding things behind the veil of National Security and that proverbial "need-to-know" lingo.

Jake crawled under the truck to attach chains to the tires. Thankfully little snow had drifted underneath. But, when he scooted out he got a cold icy shower of it down the back of his coat. Duke took the opportunity to lather his cheeks and mouth with wet-tongued affection. He wiped the canine salivary greeting from his face.

Tracy stood waving from the front door. "Do you have any thermal cups? Can I get a cup of coffee for you to go?"

He stomped the snow off his boots once he reached the porch and grabbed the shovel to clear the doorway. "Under the sideboard. Yeah, sounds great … Black is fine."

Atwood peeked his head around the open door. "How 'bout you lead the way up to the trailhead?" He leaned back in for a second and then back out of the still open door. "Miss Aspen can ride with me."

Jake pushed a shovel full of snow across the porch as Duke squeezed through the door. "Whatever she wants," he said to Atwood.

The agent tucked his head back inside and closed the door. Jake stood with shovel in hand, waiting.

A minute later Tracy came out with two thermal cups. She rolled her eyes at Jake. "My rifle in the truck?" she asked.

"Yeah."

She handed him a cup. "Let's go." With that she walked to the passenger side and climbed in.

Fumbling with his gloves and an egg sandwich, Atwood let Jake close the door behind him. "Feisty little thing isn't she?" He took a big bite of the sandwich, clicked his SUV unlocked and started the engine. "Guess I should've warmed her up and gotten the seat heaters going."

Jake pointed to the northwest. "Trail's no better than the field this time of year. I'd stay near the fence line otherwise you may find a stump or boulder that'll ruin your day."

Atwood hesitated then turned and climbed into the raised SUV.

Jake admired the winch package attached to the front, probably two grand. Sure would be nice.

•

Jake kicked snow off his boots as he climbed into the near-vintage truck. "No air conditioning, but at least the heater works good." He smiled and turned the vents toward her.

"But no seat heaters." She chuckled.

"In another lifetime maybe." He pumped the gas and eased the clutch, guiding the truck between two of the sheds and north along a rapidly disappearing fence line. Atwood kept close behind, following in Jake's tire tracks.

As he muscled the truck over snow-covered ruts, she noticed a holster under his jacket. "Packing a sidearm today?"

"My service Glock," he said." I haven't carried it in over a year—seemed like the right occasion though."

"I hope you're wrong."

They reached the fence line just south of Boxelder Gulch without incident. The blowing snow covered any evidence of their previous visit. Jake showed Atwood where the trail up to Horse Thief Ridge started. Yellow crime scene tape, half-covered by snow, flapped in the wind.

Tracy leaned across the hood of the pickup and scanned the Gulch and ridgeline through the scope of her .30-06. The warmth from the old truck stilled her apprehension about the cold and danger. Light, crisp air filled her lungs and exhaled easily.

Atwood methodically examined the spot where Stephen Kincaid had been found and repeatedly attempted to gain radiation readings to no avail. He asked Tracy to point out where the shots had come from and what vantage points they'd investigated the previous day. Jake pulled an ancient set of binoculars from behind the seat of his truck and continued to scan up and down the cloud covered rim as she and Atwood spoke.

Finally with Jake and Tracy stomping their feet to stay warm, Atwood stood on the leeward side of his SUV and pulled out his iPhone.

"It probably won't work with all the mountains around," Jake said.

Atwood glared at him deadpan and dialed. He had a connection nearly immediately. "Weather's breaking up here. How's it look coming from the north?" He nodded. "Want a flare? Well, let me know if anything changes."

He rummaged through the back of the vehicle and then climbed in the front seat, closing the door and motioning to them. In the warmth of the SUV he turned to Tracy in the backseat. "They'll be here in ten to fifteen minutes and they do want to go up on the ridge."

Jake threw his gloves into the front window dash. "We were up to the rim yesterday and Sheriff Schaffer found nothing … but this isn't about the murder, is it?"

Atwood pulled a plastic baggie from his inside coat pocket, punched the cigarette lighter, and when it popped out placed a partially smoked cigar in his mouth. He opened the window a crack and touched the red hot coil against the clipped end of the cigar. As smoke curled out through the window he inhaled forcefully until the end glowed. He blew a thin stream of smoke out the window.

Buffeting wind swirled smoke across the hood before blasting it into the sky. To the north, clouds angrily sprinted across the Black Hills and out over Rapid City. But to the south it was clearing some, a faint lull in the turbulence marching through into Minnesota and Iowa.

Atwood exhaled for the third time and nodded. "Okay, it's gonna become more and more evident as we move along today." His eyes narrowed. "Obviously we're looking for a radiation source. One that was here at the base of Horse Thief Ridge three days ago and then disappeared."

Tracy swore under her breath. "Stolen fissile material? Or a bomb?"

Atwood shrugged. He stared at the red tip of the smoldering cigar. A breeze dumped ashes onto his lap. "Yeah, that's a good question … and this is where it gets real hairy … and secret."

Jake's eyes burned with a smoldering intensity. "More secret than nuclear bombs?"

A faint rumble from the mountainside preceded a dark Air Force helicopter that swooped down on them with hurricane-like down drafts. Atwood extinguished the cigar and rolled up the window. Within a minute, the rotors throttled back. A woman and three men hunched over against the cold, and down-draft crept from the black airship toward the engulfed SUV.

The fright that gripped Tracy's stomach gave way to a battle-field-like foreboding. She knew from her combat tours that bad news generally arrived in helicopters like this. Like the time an advance squad of Special Forces had been decimated in an ambush by the Taliban, the bodies unrecoverable. That word had arrived by helicopter as well.

Atwood opened the door of the SUV as the helicopter blades idled menacingly. Tracy identified two of the men as probably Homeland Security officers. The women and other man stood erect as they approached and Tracy read the emblems on their foul-weather coats—Secret Service.

Chapter 17

Trailhead to Horse Thief Ridge

Amir had never been so cold. He ached for the warmth of his hotel room or better yet his Toronto apartment. Ten minutes in the sub-zero weather and the crappy design of the fingerless mitten/gloves was a distraction he did not need. Lying at the bottom of Boxelder Gulch under an evergreen in white tactical snow gear, he was virtually invisible. The racing helicopter passed him before he heard it coming. The down draft caught him first and he nearly ran from fright.

It was now more than a murder investigation. At a minimum, the FBI and Homeland security had become involved, along with the local and state authorities. The odds of success had just dropped. Rashid would be angry and worse yet, embarrassed. The revenging hand of Allah must not be stopped. Reprisals would be enacted. He and his family would not see Persia if the doubters did not suffer the mortal dagger to the chest.

The snow had not slowed them as he had suspected. Yet they still concentrated on the site where he had slain the stupid kid. Perhaps they knew less than he thought, time would tell. *Be patient, Amir.* Once again he risked removing the lens cover from the rifle scope. That act had revealed him the previous day. This morning though none of the group held binoculars or rifles with scopes. In fact they all stood huddled against the blowing snow on the far side of the black SUV, and now two women.

Should he risk contacting Rashid? No. Amir was on his own. The success of the jihad and the hopes of his family all lay squarely on his back. He would work his way up the side of the cliff as opportunity permitted. If he needed to shoot again the advantages of a level trajectory greatly outweighed the risks of discovery. For now it was still a murder investigation. As long as they stayed on this side of the ridge line.

•

Special Agent Rebecca McAllister stood a few inches shorter than Tracy. Complete with fur-lined parka and communications earpiece, she even had an American flag pin on her parka's left lapel. Short, thin, up-sloping eyebrows created the impression of a bird of prey. The Homeland Security Officers and a younger Secret Service agent, poorly dressed for the weather, followed her toward the SUV. She did all the talking, clearly in charge. Hard to tell her age though she appeared close to the same age as Carl Atwood, give or take a few years.

She huddled close to the open window and got right to the point with Atwood, who obviously knew her. "The body was found here at the base of the trail?"

Atwood nodded toward Jake. "Ranger ... sorry he's no longer a ranger, but was a few years back. He ranches now. Mr. Moran found him early Monday."

"Your ranch?" McAllister asked.

Jake glared at Atwood, who showed no remorse at the slip of the tongue.

"Right up to the fence line here." Jake pointed to the north and down into Boxelder Gulch. "The Kincaid Ranch borders most of the northern property line."

McAllister studied the gulch and the ascent to Horse Thief Ridge. "That was the name of the kid?"

Atwood nodded. "Yeah, Stephen Kincaid ... Warrants on the ranch and homestead are on their way." He slipped his iPhone into a leather case. "A team will be at the ranch house this morning. Unfortunately, the Sheriff has already tipped our hand by talking with the kid's parents the day of the shooting. So I don't know what we'll find there."

The Secret Service agent scrutinized Tracy in the backseat as if appraising a bug. Her lips pursed and she leaned through the window next to Atwood. "Your report mentioned aberrations in the resuscitation ... the labs were off."

A shiver ran up Tracy's spine.

Atwood's shoulder twitched.

"I was the charge nurse for the resuscitation," Tracy said.

McAllister touched her earpiece and glanced at the helicopter. "Right," she said into a wrist mounted microphone. "If you can't get back in we'll ride down with Agent Atwood." She climbed in the back seat opposite Tracy as the helicopter lifted off. "What did you notice besides the fact he was bleeding out?"

"That was probably from his low platelets, twenty thousand or so." Tracy shifted in the seat to better address the lead agent. Slight crow's feet teased the edges of her green eyes, and up close the skin on her face showed weathering. She'd done field time, not just office work. "His white blood counts were also extremely low and his electrolytes suggested he was severely dehydrated."

McAllister nodded. "How low were the white cells?"

"Right at five-hundred." A hollowness expanded out of Tracy's stomach and wrenched at her chest. She knew where this was going.

"Five to seven days post exposure," McAllister said. She stared back to the north toward the Kincaid ranch. "What were you up to, Stephen Kincaid?" She abruptly opened the door.

Snow swirled inside the SUV as the temperature plummeted. Jake stepped out beside her and a heated discussion ensued. The agent turned toward the mist covered ridge. Tracy slipped her gloves back on and again pulled the stocking cap low over her ears. As she reached for the door handle, Atwood chuckled.

"Something funny?" Tracy asked.

"He's out of his element." Atwood gestured toward Jake and the Secret Service woman with a yellow and black North Dakota State Bumblebees hat he'd pulled from the glove compartment. "She's been doing this for ten years ... nothing he says will change her mind."

"Is she with Presidential protection?"

"And counter-terrorism before that." Atwood smirked and shrugged his shoulders. "Like myself, she's never lost a member of her team ... pre-planning and well-timed execution. Otherwise things happen, like with Jake."

Tracy had seen firsthand when planning and execution went to hell in a handbasket. "Strategy and tactics."

"That's it. Know the scenario and work it by the numbers."

"You really believe that?" Tracy snorted and shook her head. "Have you ever been confronted by an overwhelming enemy force or physical conditions beyond your control?"

Atwood's face paled.

"Hopefully you'll never be in that situation, Agent. It really tests the mettle of a man ... or a woman. Mike Tyson summarized it pretty well: 'Everyone has a plan until they get hit in the face.'"

Tracy stepped out of the SUV. She hollered at Jake through the wind and motioned to the back of the truck. Reaching in, she pulled out a set of snowshoes and started strapping them on.

•

McAllister had her own agenda. Jake bit his lip. They'd surely be getting another foot of snow in the next few hours. Horse Thief Ridge was not the place to be today or, God forbid, tonight. He reluctantly backed away from Agent McAllister and knelt beside Tracy. "We were all over that area yesterday—I don't think what they're looking for is up there."

"She's going to go no matter what we say," Tracy said. "There's a lot that we don't know and no one is offering much in the way of explanations right now." She pulled the straps on the snowshoes tight across her boots. "The sooner we start the sooner we'll be back down."

The second agent, Crawford according to his name tag, and the Homeland security team, also in navy blue parkas and winter weather boots, pulled a large canvas bag behind the truck. They likewise knelt to stay out of the wind. The young skinny-faced Secret Service agent helped the Homeland Security officers with backpacks, electronics, and high-tech snowshoes. Both Homeland men could most certainly handle the load on a prolonged ascent, Henderson and Yang, one Caucasian, the other Asian or possibly a mix.

Jake threw his gear on the ground as well and started unbuckling frozen straps. "What's the Secret Service got to do with Black Hills radiation alerts?"

Crawford turned his chin slightly toward Jake and nervously

glanced up to the Homeland guys as Senior Agent McAllister rounded the SUV.

McAllister surveyed the equipment then studied Atwood through the window of the SUV. He was just completing a cell-phone call. "Atwood told me you had some questions."

The young agent handed her a set of snowshoes and chambered a magazine into an automatic assault rifle that he also handed to her.

"This is classified, of course." She nodded toward the Homeland officers who began punching through screens on a handheld GPS. Jake brushed off his hat and focused on the darkening ridgeline while he shielded his eyes from the snow with a gloved hand.

McAllister followed his glance. "Our electronics are state-of-the-art satellite controlled ... including our phones." She checked the safety on the assault rifle. "You'll both bring your rifles, right?"

"Sure ... but if we're gonna be throwing lead in someone's direction, I'd sure like to know why," Jake said.

Tracy stepped back nodding.

"So, this is how it pans out. We don't know if the source is stolen fissile material or a device."

Jake swallowed hard, trying to relieve the knot that grabbed at his throat.

She added, "The British Prime Minister is in Montreal today meeting with the Canadian Minister and his Foreign Secretary."

"We've got it, ma'am." The stockier of the two Homeland officers hefted an electronic pack onto his back as the two started toward the yellow crime scene tape snaking to and fro in the ever-increasing wind.

McAllister swung the weapon over her shoulder. "Let's talk as we climb ... it may be a long day."

Jake slipped an extra magazine into his pocket as he and Tracy shouldered their hunting rifles and followed the lead agent toward the snow-covered rim. A tightness climbed up Jake's neck to the base of his skull, trying to pull his ears down into his coat. Bret Peterson had died in the ravine just east of Horse Thief Ridge.

Chapter 18

Rim Trail to Horse Thief Ridge

Though they were slowed by the blowing and drifting snow, McAllister pushed a good pace up the switchbacks to the top of the ridge. Tracy stood with the lead agent below the outcroppings that the Sheriff and his team had examined the day before. Just below them the Homeland officers, Jake, and Atwood made their final push. Henderson's pack was over fifty pounds and Jake had insisted on bringing his complete set of climbing gear and ropes. Back in the SUV, the toasty warm Scott Crawford acted as base support.

Braced on the same rock she'd used the day before, Tracy scanned Boxelder Gulch and the crests to the north and south for any incongruities. She'd done this three times during the ascent as had Jake. Snow flurries had largely made it a futile effort. Hopefully that would help hide them as well. Certainly the intermittent cloud cover on the ridge would protect them some. Could also hurt the search for whatever they were after.

Tracy rested the stock of her rifle on the snow-covered trail as Jake joined them. "So what's the connection with the British and Canadian Prime Ministers?" she asked.

McAllister kicked her snowshoes against a boulder and drank from a thermos as the Homeland officers negotiated the last of the switchbacks. "They're flying to Vancouver the Saturday after Christmas but will stop over in Rapid City to meet with the President ... at Mount Rushmore."

The color drained from Tracy's face. Jake closed his eyes and shook his head.

McAllister nodded as she rubbed her fingers across dry lips.

"Exactly, so we have forty-eight hours to get this figured out or the spontaneous Middle East planning meeting is going somewhere else."

"What is it you're expecting to find up here?" Tracy waved her hand across the pine- and rock-strewn landscape. "Certainly the snow is not going to obscure a gamma source strong enough to register on portal monitors and to cause acute radiation sickness."

Henderson handed McAllister the GPS monitor as he trudged up the last few steps to join the group. He eased the pack to the ground and squatted on his haunches as Yang and the lead agent manipulated the map coordinates, zooming in and out.

"Crawford is actually the team's physicist." She held the GPS and faced east. "Mount Rushmore is just a little south of due east from here ... three-quarters of a mile as the crow flies. Do the trails lead to the summit above the monument?"

"That's National Park Service land," Tracy said.

Jake sighed deeply. "Yeah, but the trails do join up. And you can get access all the way to the cliff face above the monument."

"I've never been over that far," Tracy said.

Jake repeatedly snapped and unsnapped a clamp attached to his climbing equipment. A hawk or eagle of some sort coasted on the wind currents between them and the adjacent crest.

"Lot of steep cliffs." Jake's eyes rose to the sky. "The trails can get real slippery with ice and snow—even when they're just wet." He held the .270 casually aimed toward the ground.

Atwood stretched his back in an accentuated twist and then pulled up the rain gear and fleece he wore. Checking access to his gun, Tracy figured. The black back of his hat and Thinsulate hoodie gave way to a bright yellow bumblebee caricature on the front when he turned toward her. Probably had a son or daughter attending school in Fargo.

"Well, Crawford says the source is either shielded with lead or buried under several feet of rock, maybe both." McAllister sent Henderson and Yang across the face of the ridge with one of the Geiger counters. They returned with a negative report.

She reluctantly turned to the northwest.

Tracy followed her gaze. "Oh geez, if we're going we'd better get it done quick. That storm is bearing down on us with no mercy."

"Keep one of the counters out," Yang said. "Never know when

we might come across something."

"Great." Jake was now slamming the magazine into his gloved hand.

He was upset. This was far from the controlled situations he was used to. It was more like what she'd experienced the past year.

He bit his lower lip. "You get us to the Park Service land and I'll get us to the summit above the monuments."

"Is it dangerous?" McAllister asked.

"Not the way I'm gonna take you," Jake said. "We go in and we come out the same way … all together. Got it?"

Everyone nodded, except Atwood.

•

Clearly they were going over the ridge and would in all likelihood continue on toward the Presidents' monument. Amir had climbed nearly to the edge of the rim and had burrowed under a snow-covered spruce when the Homeland officers came in his direction. Three sparrows had shrieked away, certainly exposing him. But no, the men were too intent on their instruments.

Fifty meters up the trail and they would be in his firing line. He did not want to have to engage the officers. Already suspicions were high. More shootings would absolutely compromise the mission, still preferable to straight-forward failure.

Sweat trickled down the back of his shoulders despite the cold. Climbing the rough terrain off the trail stained his worn knees and resulted in scrapes and abrasions. The altitude did not bother him, this was nothing. His heartbeat returned to a slow pace within a minute of reaching the crest.

He'd not scouted this part of the ridge. The best concealment and shooting lanes would take time to determine. He didn't have that benefit. They'd be over the crest and into the pine forest. He would lose his opportunity.

Just across the ridge he found a rock outcropping with two fallen trees that formed a natural tripod. Praise Allah. He would be shooting down slightly, luckily though his sight line would be unobstructed. A clear shot to a switchback they'd be on within minutes of starting their descent down this side. The range was close to one-hundred and fifty meters, and the drop would be only a couple of inches. Aiming a little high would compensate for that. He mumbled a prayer for clouds and fog to stay away.

The minute or two that he had to wait should be used to calm his heart beat and nerves. Slow his breathing and prepare mentally for the rapid fire he would need to ensure any level of success with six-to-one odds. He barely thought of the two women he would soon kill.

•

The cliff where Bret Peterson died lay a thousand yards across the ravine. They would walk within spitting distance of where Jake had spent nearly an hour performing CPR on the young man. He'd been to Horse Thief Ridge a few times these past few years but not into this ravine that held so many dark memories.

"The snow seems less over here."

Tracy's voice pulled Jake's thoughts away from that catastrophic rescue.

"We're still gonna need the snowshoes though." Henderson led the way a few steps in front of Tracy.

Jake took up the rear, stopping every few minutes to sweep the ravine and east facing ridge with the binoculars.

Clouds completely obscured the northern ridge now and might soon be upon them as well. He'd found his way through this part of the Park before in near whiteout circumstances. He could do it again, if it came to that, but it would take a long time—maybe until after nightfall. Never good, being delayed on a snow-covered mountainside at night.

The climb to the Mount Rushmore ridge was technically not difficult, though inexperienced climbers could get in trouble just about anywhere. Jake had learned that several times, and the fact ultimately led to his downfall. Tracy directed the Homeland officers and correctly warned them when conditions were marginal.

Three white-tail deer sprinted down the ravine silently, their distinctive white tails evaporating into the whipped snow. Tracy had spotted them first and smiled at Jake as he lowered his scope from following the leaping animals. She had a wonderful, honest smile, inviting without conditions. Ah, he remembered the kisses from the night before.

Jake sensed the clearing of clouds from Horse Thief Ridge before he turned into the increasing brightness. Scope to his eye he picked up movement just below the crest. "Movement," he whispered harshly. "Fifty yards below the ridge line and couple hundred yards out."

A leafless aspen partially blocked his view. Shots rang out. The "pop" from behind him registered just as the rock in front of him splintered. Soldiers experienced in warfare probably reacted quicker to threats. The whistle of a bullet to his far right and the guttural exhalation from Yang behind him signaled the deadliness of the attack.

Tracy fired back up the mountain. No other return fire sounded until his .270 recoiled and his fingers flew through ejecting and rechambering a round. His second shot was followed by silence except for two more shots from Tracy. The sulfur smell of gunpowder hung heavy in the air.

Chapter 19

Horse Thief Ridge, Black Hills

The first two shots were unanswered. His third shot jerked high when he reacted to the muzzle flash and crack of a high-velocity round against the rock above him. A good start, Amir decided, nearly halfway finished. Something tugged at his mind though. A flash of yellow as he'd squeezed off the third shot.

In the back hall at the Toronto Mosque, Rashid had ended their last conversation with a ringed hand on his shoulder and a whisper. "Shoot nothing yellow."

"What?" Amir had asked, perplexed after all the intricate planning. "Shoot nothing yellow? What does that mean?"

Rashid had been infuriated but stoic in his reply. "You heard ... now go with Allah"

He withdrew behind the fallen tree as he chambered the forth round. Had he just made an awful mistake? Time to think of that later. He rotated to fire again. A searing cut through his right hip and spun him to the ground. Blood clearly spotted the snow behind him. A hot poker burned from his right hip to his foot.

He could not be taken alive. With three functioning limbs he slung the rifle across his back and scrambled up to the ridgeline protected by the rock outcropping. He recalled little of the frantic scramble back down to Boxelder Gulch and was relieved to see the lack of response from the vehicles at the trailhead.

A clear trail of blood would allow easy tracking for the next half hour—after that it would likely be covered with the newly fallen snow. The entrance wound was small but below his right kidney a fist-size hole oozed too much to be ignored. Amir stripped off his left glove and grimacing from pain wedged it into his flank. He could not lift his right foot, but by shuffling sideways, he could drag it fairly well. His off-road motorcycle was hidden a mere two hundred meters up the frozen creek bed.

All hell would break loose now. He needed to go to ground and soon.

•

Henderson hit the ground in a splatter of red and white, and never moved. Tracy dove off the trail and swung her rifle toward the ridge. Yang twisted, grabbing a collapsing leg. McAllister spun to her right and ended up across Tracy's legs, just as she returned the first shots directed toward an area of boulders and fallen trees.

Her first shot went high and then she heard shots from her left as she re-chambered and fired twice more. As quickly as it started all was silent. Except for the gasps of Officer Yang.

"Jake, cover me. I need to get Yang out of the line of fire." She sensed his position up and to her left.

"Okay. Go, go, go." He fired twice up into the tree line as Tracy and McAllister pulled Yang off the trail beside them. Tracy flipped her backpack on the ground and within seconds had gauze and pressure dressings out. McAllister split Yang's pants up to his mid-thigh, exposing a ragged, thankfully not pumping, wound with bone projecting out.

Jake called. "Got him?"

"Yeah."

"What about Henderson and McAllister?"

McAllister held pressure on Yang's leg as Tracy unwrapped dressing material.

"I'm fine," the Secret Service agent said. "Henderson's dead."

"Where is Atwood?" McAllister asked.

"He's below me to the left," Jake said.

"Are you hit," Tracy asked.

"Who?" Jake asked. "Me or Atwood?"

"Either of you?"

"I'm fine. Isn't Atwood down by you?"

Tracy raised her head cautiously and peered first up to the ridge and then rapidly swept the mountainside. "He's laying across the trail to your left ... I don't think he's moving."

"Okay, I'll try to move back down to him." Jake inched down the trail on his stomach and then rolled behind a rock next to the motionless Atwood. He grimaced across the trail at Tracy. "I count only one," Jake said. "Like yesterday."

She avoided the bloodied body of Henderson and rolled reck-lessly through snow and rock to Jake's side. Atwood lay crumpled between a tree and rock outcropping, his Bumblebees hat and semi-automatic Glock several feet away. Blood trickled from a lin-ear tear in his black hoodie just above his left eye.

A cell phone fell from inside Atwood's coat when Jake turned him on his back. Jake slipped it in his own coat pocket and re-trieved the Glock.

Tracy lifted the unconscious agent's eyelids to inspect his pu-pils.

Jake ejected the magazine from Atwood's gun and pulled back the receiver, catching the forty-caliber round that flew from the gun barrel.

At the clicking of the pistol slide, Atwood's eyes bolted open and he flailed his arms, blood collecting in his left eye.

Tracy literally sat on the agent's chest to keep him from stand-ing up. Reeking gasps of mint and tobacco blew in her face. "Carl. Carl. Stay down!" She took both his cheeks in her hand and forced his adrenaline-injected eyes to focus on hers. "You're fine, Carl. You've been grazed but the bleeding is already stopping. Do you understand me?"

Atwood blinked. Blood matted his forehead but he seemed to refocus. He scrunched his eyes in pain and then nodded. "Okay. Right ... can you get off of me?"

Jake scanned the ridge, condensation from deep breaths hang-ing like Santa's beard about his face. "This is stupid. We're sitting ducks out here. And now he's probably gone again ... like yester-day."

She crawled off Atwood, her bounding pulse trying to return to normal.

Dumbfounded, Atwood gaped at McAllister and then at Hen-derson's body, wiped blood from his eye, and mumbled something unintelligible.

Jake handed him the unloaded pistol, bullet and magazine. The sulfur odor of a recently fired bullet tickled Tracy's nostrils reminiscent of cold Afghan hillsides.

McAllister held pressure on Yang's leg while blood trickled down her left arm.

"You've been hit too," Tracy said.

"No. I landed on a broken tree limb when I dove off the trail." McAllister rubbed snow across the wound.

Tracy crawled back over to the two and turned Yang's leg slightly left and right. "You were lucky. No major bleeding ... must have missed the artery." She washed the blood from her hands with snow and wiped them on her pants. "I've got stuff in my bag to get a pressure dressing on that ... It's gonna hurt, but with a little work it'll be fine." She tried to give the officer a reassuring smile.

Yang nodded through clenched teeth, then looked over at Henderson. "Damn! What now?" he asked.

McAllister tore a bandage out of Tracy's pack and unceremoniously slapped it on her left arm. "We go on ... Obviously somebody doesn't want us up on that summit anytime soon."

"And if we don't get to the summit today," Tracy said. "It may have to wait till spring."

A large stain of blood covered Henderson's chest and back flowing out onto the sterile white snow. Ironically, the thought that hit Tracy was how much easier recovering Henderson's body would be as compared to a Marine killed in Helmand Province. The notification of next of kin would be no easier though.

"He ran yesterday," Tracy said to McAllister. "As soon as he shot and we shot back, he skedaddled."

Jake pointed a couple hundred yards down the ravine. "Those trees would shield us from the ridge if we can get into the tree line just past that split down the ravine. The rim trail to the monument is about a hundred and fifty feet above ... and the terrain is reasonable."

Tracy leaned next to Yang. "Can you make it into the trees? We can help you."

"I'll make it," he said a stony set to his jaw replacing the earlier grimaces.

"He has to," Agent McAllister said, frowning. "He's our bomb expert."

Jake covered the four as they dragged Yang up out of sight. Despite emptying a magazine of rounds into the trees not a single shot was returned. A few ricochets off the boulders echoed into the ravines, but no return fire. Tracy and Atwood covered Jake's zigzag run to the trees in a similar one-sided gun fight.

•

They'd dragged Yang up the Ponderosa Pine and snow-covered slope to the rim trail before Jake realized he'd run directly past the cliff Bret Peterson had fallen from. A bruised elbow and wet snow down the back of his jacket were the only things that bothered him—besides Henderson's death.

"No activity in any of these areas," Atwood reported as he waved the receiver of the Geiger counter through a 360-degree arc. The torn hoodie, pulled at an angle to the left, had succeeded in stemming the blood flow from his forehead.

McAllister squatted next to Yang and adjusted the GPS. "Half mile still … You're no good for that."

Yang stoically repositioned his bandaged leg as he fingered from screen to screen on his iPad. "The images are better now," he said. "I've got good reception here and you'll have it on the rim too. Post me up the hillside with the MP5 and I'll be constantly available on the sat phone. First thing is we need to find the source and quick. I'd just slow you down."

Atwood nodded.

McAllister pushed the stocking cap back on her head. "What if it's a device with a motion trigger?"

"What are the odds of that?" Yang handed her the iPad. "I've never seen a personal carried weapon with a motion trigger—not even in suicide bombers. Besides if you find a device, a motion sensor is generally easy to spot." He grabbed back the iPad and with four or five finger flicks had a schematic in front of him. "Keep this document loaded in and examine the device to see if it has any long tubes running the length of the frame or something that resembles a carpenter's level … but trust me you won't find that."

"I wish I had your confidence. We'll check-in every five." She handed him the automatic rifle and an extra magazine. "Where do you want to camp out?"

He pointed to three white spruce trees just below a stand of aspen. Atwood and Jake helped him settle under the snow-covered limbs and added extra branches for camouflage.

The beauty and fresh smell of the forest still brought pleasant memories to Jake. It was difficult to pair violent death and massive, hateful destruction with the pristine landscape.

"Stunning, isn't it." Tracy stood behind him. "There is nothing like this in Afghanistan ... and yet the Islamic extremists fight for every square mile."

"I guess it makes sense for them to destroy the best of America."

Her golden eyes bore deep in to him. "Not my home."

Tracy's expression said it all. The bittersweet love of country, earned and kept free by the blood of thousands of patriots. The last one being Officer James Henderson of Fargo, North Dakota.

Chapter 20

Hiking Trails and Valleys West of Mount Rushmore

Special Agent McAllister stayed on her satellite phone continuously for the fifteen-minute ascent to the staging area above Mount Rushmore. Sheriff Schaffer had three deputies and numerous state agencies triangulating on all routes out of Boxelder Gulch. Crawford had heard shots from over the ridgeline yet had seen no activity in or around the Moran or Kincaid ranches.

Yang had seen no activity and reported the bandage remained tight with minimal bleeding. He did mention that the Geiger counters may have to be within fifty feet of a device to get significant levels of gamma radiation. Minot Air Base reported the weather was worsening and they didn't think they could get any air support in before late Christmas day.

McAllister stared at her cell phone. "Technology—craps out when you need it the most."

"Hey, like the Marines, we've got boots on the ground ... and that counts for a lot." Tracy swung a 360-degree survey with the rifle scope. "So far so good." She removed her snowshoes as the windswept stone summit had little snow except the deep drifts against north-facing rocks.

McAllister pointed to a concrete slab the size of a small house and derrick-type rusted-steel structures. "I take it that was one of the staging areas for the monument construction?"

Jake walked with one of the Geiger counters toward the rusting structure. "Right, this crane sits right above Jefferson and Roosevelt."

"What type of bomb could reasonably be carried up here?" Tracy asked.

Atwood smirked and nodded at McAllister, who busied herself expanding the GPS map to include the cities of Keystone and Rapid City.

Finished probing the device, McAllister rubbed her gloved hands together. "Well, Yang and the Homeland people think a backpack nuke like the Russian RA-115s would be most likely. According to Stanislav Lunev, the Soviets successfully squeezed a five kiloton weapon into a fifty- to sixty-pound pack the size of a bag of golf clubs."

"Really, a Russian 115?" Nausea gripped Tracy as she flashed to a burned-out forward-aid station in Helmand Province—the raped and injured Arab, or perhaps Persian, girl. "And it would take out all of Mount Rushmore?"

"And contaminate a large area if they succeeded in lacing the device with isotopes like Strontium or Cobalt."

Jake approached the end of the concrete slab and leaned precariously over the cliff side of the monument, eddies of windblown snow funneled up from below.

"You mean a 'dirty bomb," Tracy said.

"Or a combination of both ... which unfortunately is possible with today's technology." McAllister stopped punching numbers into her phone, rubbed her fingers, and focused on Jake. "What's he doing?"

Tracy followed her gaze. Jake stood near the weathered metal derrick, waving his arms as he unloaded climbing gear from his backpack. "I think he's found something."

The two women and Atwood joined Jake on the slab where the wind mercilessly pummeled them, whipping hoods and scarfs like exuberant flags.

Jake busily wrapped climbing ropes around the base of the derrick. "The Geiger counter gets progressively more gamma signal the closer I get to the edge."

"You think a device could be somewhere on the monument?" Atwood asked as the counter he held ticked faster the closer he came to the derrick and cliff edge.

"You're going to rappel down ... in this weather?" Tracy asked as darker and darker clouds rolled in from the northwest, out of Alberta and Saskatchewan.

Jake put his hand out to Atwood. "Give me your satellite phone. I'll need it for communication."

Atwood hesitated just a second and then unclipped the carrier from his belt and pulled his gloves off to attach the phone and holder to Jake's belt. "Government equipment and all—you understand."

Jake braced himself at the top of the monument. Slacked the rope a bit and double checked the D ring just in front of his stomach. With a wave he began his descent but not before saying to Atwood, "You know, I don't work for the government anymore."

Tracy wasn't sure if Jake was smiling at Atwood as he went over the side or grimacing at the cold wind blowing in his face. She wrapped the safety line he'd handed her around another rung of the derrick and slowly played it out as Jake descended.

•

Amir's hand felt numb. Switching the gloves every few minutes had worked at first but now the sensation had not returned to his left hand even after leaving the glove on for nearly five minutes. The biting cold, accentuated by the speed of the mountain bike, had frozen the blood-soaked glove stuffed in the right-hip wound. The bleeding had eased, at least outwardly.

Coming to a rutted junction in the mining road, he attempted to down shift but was unable to flex his right foot. Stomping and pulling on the gear shift with his heel caused shocks to shoot up his thigh and buttock. Finally he managed to shift. Tears froze on his cheek each time he went through the motion. The knobbed tires gripped well on the fluffy snow. Thankfully no ice yet.

At the crest of the hill, blowing snow swirled under the helmet faceplate. He felt nothing, his cheeks and nose completely numb since shortly after he'd left the concealed ravine.

The Americans had unfortunately been alerted. The meeting would be canceled and the ultimate fatal blow would not be delivered. A hope remained though, perhaps Amir's glorious attack and the winter storm conjured by Allah would still allow the flaming sword of revenge to slice deep into the heartland of the Zionist dogs. Laying waste to one of their most sacred sites for centuries to come.

To the left a weather-washed road led higher into the foothills, the right back toward Rapid City. He could not be captured. No, he needed another seventy-two hours. The jihad must succeed. Gritting his teeth, he pulled up with all his might on the right leg gear shift. A click sounded. "Allah be praised."

Five more minutes—ten at the most—and he'd be to the abandoned mine shaft where he'd given the bomb to Stephen Kincaid. The boy had been excited about destroying the monument. He had not been told about the Plutonium 240 and Cobalt 60. Contaminating the western United States for a hundred years might not have excited him so much.

Spruce trees on the north-slope signaled his approach to the mine. A rabbit cut across his path and nearly sent him over the edge of a particularly rocky section. Though it appeared pleasantly snow covered, the rugged rocks would break and maim him with any fall. The vibration of the motorcycle and the freezing onslaught left only a dull ache where the high-powered round had sliced through his pelvis. It was a bad wound ... maybe mortal. That was in Allah's hands. Amir needed only get to the mine and conceal himself until the wrath of the Creator had descended.

Finally, he throttled back and rolled to the boarded-up shaft. He did not have the key to the lock. It shattered with a single shot from the .30-06. The recoil of the rifle sent a shock down his leg that brought spots to his eyes. Pulling hastily at the boards he made enough room to push the mountain bike through and deep enough into the mine to not be visible from the outside. Quickly he pulled the boards back in place and wrapped the chain as best possible.

Pushing and pulling the motorcycle, he struggled by the headlamp beam as deep as he could into the shaft. Fifty or so feet in he had to abandon the machine, exhausted and his way blocked by uneven rock and wedged lumber. His leg dragged as he crawled over broken support beams, now with only the fading light of the motorcycle headlamp. Finally, he settled on the dirt mound of a collapsed wall. He had put nearly fifteen miles between himself and the Gulch. They would never find him in time. He drank from the goatskin water bladder, a gift from his wife at the birth of their daughter. The solitary keepsake had been his companion through wars, famine, and many too many weeks away from his beloved Haifa.

A few days and he could attempt to make the Canadian border. A long trip in winter but his Haifa waited in Toronto, just a few days, a few days to ensure the explosion. He would surely feel or hear it, though he was having trouble feeling his legs and the shaft was so cold. Even through the winter survival gear the cold gnawed at his bones. That was not good—he couldn't last three days in this state. He would rest some and then make his next plan.

As he closed his eyes he felt a warmth in his chest that expanded to a bright sun over Persia. He sat on the bank of a flowing river, majestic in blue and green. Across the river Haifa with baby in her arms beckoned him from a stand of lush reeds and water-lilies. With a glowing smile she climbed white marble stairs to a radiant building topped with golden domes. Pausing at the top step, framed in flowers, she again beckoned, turned, and entered a stout jeweled door with rays of sunlight splashing all about.

Gently he placed his foot in the river, warmth and sensation returned to his feet and legs. Slowly he eased into the flowing current. Sweetness enveloped him as a swirl of light transported him into the miraculous presence of his Haifa and all his ancestors.

Chapter 21

Mount Rushmore

Rappelling down the face of Mount Rushmore had been relatively easy. Many cliffs in the Black Hills were far more technical and hazardous.

The bite of the Canadian storm abated as soon as Jake left the summit. If the day had cooperated and laid some sunshine across the face of Mount Rushmore, the climb might have actually been a pleasant outing. He'd often dreamed of climbing the monument but except for the rare cleaning or repair chores such activities were not in the Park Service's plan.

He kicked himself for not switching out Atwood's phone with McAllister's ear piece before launching over the summit. Halfway down he punched in Yang, who by holding the phone next to his mouthpiece, effectively connected McAllister as well, though Yang had to continuously repeat Jake's conversation.

"Geiger counter is steadily increasing in activity," Jake said.

"Roger that. Increasing gamma signal," Yang said. "I'll bet they've laced the bitch with Cobalt or other trash isotopes they were able to get their hands on."

"Has to be some shielding or the counter would be going bat-shit by now," McAllister added in a tight whisper.

The belaying harness held Jake's buttocks and thighs comfortably as he pocketed the phone and continued his descent. Just below the stony projection of Jefferson's hair, Jake spotted a glimmer of metal coming from a split in the rock behind the President's jaw and near the back wall of the monument. His heart hammered against his rib cage.

"I got what looks like metal tubing tucked back in a crevice behind the Jefferson head."

"How is the gamma radiation?" Yang asked as Jake held his left hand in the brake position and wrapped his right hand, with the phone, around the descent line.

"Starting to peg out on the lower scale."

"Definitely a plutonium device." Yang grunted and inhaled in a staccato of pain. "Can you get a picture of the device and send it to me?"

Jake peered into the split in the rock and did not see any leveling-type equipment or instrumentation. At an acute angle he could see a digital counter with six numbers slowly changing. After nearly three minutes of maneuvering across the cliff face, finally he had a reasonably clear picture to transmit.

"Coming at you," he said to Yang. "I got three long cylinders with an aluminum frame … It's wedged in pretty good but I think I can get a loop of the safety line around it and with a little help pull it free."

"Wait," Yang said calmly. "Give me a couple of minutes."

Jake hung between the mammoth sculptures of Jefferson and Roosevelt. Even after five years of living with the monument daily he was awestruck by the proximal presence of these icons of the American past. Deep breaths of moist fresh mountain air slowed the pounding in his chest.

He was brought back with stark reality when Yang came back on the line.

"Does the device feel warm?" Yang asked without inflection, as if reading from a manual.

Jake removed a glove and leaned into the crevice. The aluminum frame felt cold to the touch as did the metal cylinders. He hoped that was good news.

"Everything feels cold."

"Good." The timber of the agent's voice had risen an octave as if he'd just been told he'd been promoted. "I think we can go on with getting it up to the summit." Yang's voice faded in and out as he apparently juggled instruments. "—or tubular structure within the frame."

Apparently Yang felt confident the device had no motion-detonation component.

"Roger, I read no motion components." Jake took the lack of any response to the contrary as confirmation. "Okay, I'm going to get a line around this baby and get the heck out of Dodge."

"Looks like the timer has quite awhile to go yet." Yang was clearer now. "I'd just keep an eye on how fast it seems the numbers are progressing."

"You mean, let you know if it suddenly starts spinning like an out-of-control top," Jake said.

"Yeah, steady as she goes is the best scenario." Yang sounded preoccupied.

"Right, Tonto." The spinning top thing apparently was not a good omen. In fact, Jake remembered some James Bond movie where that exact misfortune had happened, with a nuclear bomb.

The ascent went fairly well, though despite warnings, Jake had a difficult time keeping the device even remotely level. He doubted anyone could have done so while originally positioning the bomb.

"Weight seems about right," Tracy said as the metal-framed device and Jake eased back up to the concrete slab. "It must have been an all-day job for Kincaid to get that up here to the summit and then down the face of the monument—he'd have had to do that at night, I imagine."

McAllister held the Geiger counter right against one of the metal cylinders. "Yeah, somehow the Kincaid kid must have unshielded the source somewhere along the line for him to get so sick, so fast."

"Curiosity killed the cat," Atwood said.

No one laughed.

Tracy hugged Jake and in the process got caught in his climbing harness. A spark in her amber eyes penetrated him deeply. A slight moistness, not quite a tear, wetted the top of her cheek.

"I'm fine," he said, untangling her from the nylon straps and holding her at arm's length. Atwood shuffled his feet across the deteriorating concrete. Jake's chest heaved involuntarily as Tracy helped him out of the climbing gear. Relief flooded over him as the straps loosened. Her warm breath on his neck felt natural and reassuring.

"Let's get this back down to Yang." McAllister nodded toward Atwood who grabbed the other end of the frame.

The digital counter continued, slow and uninterrupted.

Tracy tipped her chin to the northern sky and blew a frosty breath into the wind. "No one is flying in here today."

McAllister touched her earphone and added, "Nuclear disposal technicians and an Explosive Ordinance Team are on the move by truck from Minot as we speak."

"And when do you expect them?" Jake asked.

McAllister gently set the bomb down and pushed her hat off her brow. "Probably won't be till early morning."

"Yang doesn't do disarming?" Tracy's face scrunched around tight lips.

"We came in from Rapid City. The disposal teams didn't make the window out of Minot." McAllister slid her sat phone into a Velcro sealed pocket. "Our helicopter is still in Rapid City but as you can see … no one is flying anywhere north of here, except hurricane hunters."

Snow-covered ice made the descent tricky, especially muscling the sixty-plus-pound bomb between the four of them, and at the same time helping Yang avoid a painful fall. Below the summit of Horse Thief Ridge they took about fifteen minutes covering Officer Henderson's body with rocks. Jake wedged a long branch down into the pile with Henderson's hat on top for recovery identification. In six hours, this makeshift burial site would be covered for the winter.

Surprisingly, Tracy produced a bird feather and respectfully placed it at the base of the branch. She mumbled a few lines of a rhythmic chant and blew the remnants of a crushed pinecone across the burial mound. Though not a formal ceremony, she probably felt obligated in these sacred hills to give Henderson's soul some direction to a peaceful afterlife. His sacrifice deserved that.

Agent Crawford spotted for them and gave coverage during their three-hour traverse to Horse Thief Ridge and descent down to the vehicles. Jake had little confidence in the young physicist's shooting ability, so he and Tracy took turns posting coverage for the other three who toted the bomb and assisted Yang. Carrying a sixty-pound bomb through three feet of snow while wearing snowshoes and assisting Yang was like repeating Ranger School.

Despite the cold, sweat ran down Jake's back as he rested at the bottom of the descent and studied the nuclear device sitting in the bed of his truck. "This ol' rattletrap will shake the dickens out of that if we go very far."

"No, the less we move it the better," Yang said as McAllister and Atwood helped him into the back of the SUV.

It turned out to not be a problem—especially since it took them another hour and a half, and three dig-outs of the truck and SUV, before they got the half-mile to the ranch house.

The darkness of an overcast night in the rugged mountains shrouded the vehicles as Jake eventually made out the yard light.

It seemed as if he'd been gone a week.

Chapter 22

Moran Ranch, Black Hills of South Dakota

"We're gonna sit tight here till the cavalry arrives." McAllister sipped coffee and stood within eyesight of the bomb, still in the bed of Jake's truck, tucked into the doorless shed across from the ranch house.

Tracy refilled Atwood's and Crawford's cups with coffee as her loyal companion, Duke, strayed from her leg only when she stopped and only long enough to sniff the truck, bomb and new arrivals. "I hope that cavalry has a medic with them. I'll redress Yang's wound with what Jake has in the house but it's gonna take some serious debridement and frequent dressing changes, probably surgery." She noticed the eagle feather hanging in the front window of the Ford. She reached through the window and slipped the feather and leather strap off the mirror.

Crawford stared at a bulky multi-gadgeted watch that dwarfed his skinny left wrist. "Tell Yang the digital display is still counting slowly ... looks to me like its counting seconds. With that we've still got a couple of days."

"Sounds about right," McAllister said. The aluminum frame "thudded" as she snapped it with her finger. Duke scooted back nearly between Tracy's legs.

"Yang doing okay?" The agent raised an eyebrow at Tracy and then held her iPhone high above her head slowly rotating, checking bars for reception.

"Jake's getting some peroxide and clean dressings together. He'll do through the night, I guess." Tracy pushed a dangling string of hair behind her ear. Exhaustion pulled at her shoulders and the throbbing in her feet rivaled a toothache.

"You both were good help today," McAllister said.

"Enough excitement for awhile." Tracy stared out at the dime-sized flakes accentuated by the ranch yard light. "So we just sit and wait. Any periphery set?"

McAllister chuckled. "Ever the soldier ... we're not in Afghanistan." She rechecked her 9 mm HK and glanced at three black boxes on the back of Jake's truck. "Motion detectors—two hundred yards out to the north and east. Crawford set them just after we pulled in."

A veil of snow reflected from the light beam.

"Yeah." Crawford followed her gaze. "I had to tweak the sensitivity some with all the wind and flurries."

McAllister stepped to the door with Crawford and Tracy. "No terrorist group has ever mounted a frontal assault on federal agents within the continental U. S." She squinted into the snowy and dark Dakota night. "The Kincaid Ranch detachment got a weak signal over the septic tank. They elected not to dig it up. His mother says he's been sick with vomiting and diarrhea for at least four days." She rubbed her hands forcefully across her eyes and forehead. "His dad says he converted to Islam while in Toronto."

Tracy nodded. It was always the young who paid the price of war. She eased out through the entry, followed by Duke. As the wind stung her neck she turned back to McAllister. "What's this mean for the President's summit and all?"

"Cancelled," McAllister said, as she glanced up from punching the face of the iPhone. "Rumor has it Jackson Hole will be the site, but no one is telling the Canadians yet. The leak was most likely on their end."

Tracy kept her face turned away from the stinging cold as she slogged through the accumulating snow in the ranch yard. The fresh crisp smell competed with an earthy whiff of hay bales as the breezes out of the north continued to throw flurries their way. She leaned in a partially open window of the SUV. "Jake says he's got a space-heater and extension cord in the storage shed if you get tired of hanging out in the Tahoe."

Atwood gave her a thumbs up as he sipped coffee and massaged his left temple. The lone yard light cut a shadow across his face, accentuating his prominent nose like a cartoon villain. "You could grab those and a blanket and bunk in here with me if you'd like to stay warm."

Duke stood back two paces, hackles up, snow accumulating on his eyebrows artificially aging him several years.

"You all gonna take turns watching the bomb ... or is that a Secret Service job?" Tracy ducked her chin as a swirl of snow blew off the shed onto the Tahoe. Duke grudgingly retreated another pace.

"Whatever they want." Atwood blinked at the flurries, pulled the collar of his coat up and scrunched his neck against the cold. He hesitated. "How's Jake taking Henderson's killing?"

"What do you mean?"

"You know ... it seems like every time he's on an outing into the Park somebody gets killed." Atwood shrugged his shoulder and held Tracy's gaze.

Heat replaced the chill in her neck. "You ass. If not for Jake, you and Miss Secret Service might also be glassy-eyed and covered with snow right now yourself." She pushed away from the window. Duke took two silent steps toward the SUV.

"Whoa! Didn't mean to tweak your ever-loving soul, soldier." Atwood held his palms up to the window. "I just don't know if I'd be climbing into those hills with Ranger Moran anytime in the near future, if I had my choice."

Through the curtain-less front window of the house, Tracy saw the sandy-blond waves of Jake's hair bounce as he worked the first-aid dressing off Yang. What was the Park Service thinking? What a loss.

"Yeah, it's all about your choices, isn't it, Carl?" Tracy's heartbeat slowed as she walked behind the SUV. She ran into guys like him from time to time. They all got theirs eventually or died alone in some apartment in a big city.

She patted Duke's head and scratched lightly behind his ear as he released from his sentry stance and followed her to the house.

Henderson's death was no way Jake's fault. Probably not the young ranger's either, though she didn't know for sure. Her chest throbbed for Jake's anguish, and the heartache he must have to endure when dealing with jerks like Carl Atwood. Taking a deep breath she pushed open the heavy front door.

A deluge of swirling snow followed her and Duke into the room. "Sorry," she said as Yang, lying on the sole couch, cringed against the cold.

Jake stuffed bloody gauze into a plastic bag. "I don't see an exit wound," he said. "The bullet is still in there."

"Yeah, I think the femur stopped it." Tracy leaned over and examined the undressed bullet hole with white shards of bone projecting from a laceration just above the entry site. "Bleeding's under control though ... You got anything for pain. And what about antibiotics?"

"I've got a few Zithromax left from bronchitis last fall." Jake bounded up the stairs. "Just Aleve and Tylenol for pain I'm afraid." She shouted up the stairs, "Bring both. The Aleve actually is pretty good for bone pain ... any strong alcohol?"

"I've got some Bailey's Irish Cream Whisky in the refrigerator. Makes a good night cap."

"Well, that would probably be good for us right about now but we better keep—" She walked back to Yang. "What's your first name?"

"Linn," he said with a grimace. "I go by Hank though."

She nodded. "Right. Hank needs to keep an empty stomach in case they decide to operate tonight or in the morning."

Yang stoically took deep, measured breaths through the peroxide rinse and redressing. Duke sat silently on his rug observing every action and reaction. Luckily, Jake had found some out-of-date hydrocodone from a root canal years earlier.

Twenty minutes later the pain medicines kicked in. Tracy and Jake took medicinal advantage of the Bailey's with coffee. Duke dove into an evening bowl of Purina.

Nine-thirty. The Air Force technicians and medic would be at least another five hours. The wind periodically rattled the storm shutters—mostly on the upstairs windows.

"If you want to check on McAllister and those folks," She yawned, "I'm gonna lay down upstairs for a bit."

She looked from Jake to Yang who lay with his hands across his chest, eyes closed and breathing slow and regular. She picked up the eagle feather from the table where she'd laid it and set it gently on the sofa next to Yang's leg. After all, this was Lakota land.

Jake swallowed the last of his coffee and started pulling on his boots. "I would think it'd be a little hard to sleep with a ticking nuclear bomb outside your door."

Tracy scoffed. She'd seen her share of gallows humor in hospitals and of course in the war. "Heck of an alarm clock." Her thighs muscles tightened as she climbed the stairs. She'd probably leave off the hiking and climbing tomorrow.

◆

Apparently she could sleep through a nuclear occurrence. Jake watched Tracy doze by the light of the hallway. Her soft complexion and innocent beauty appeared much as they had a decade ago. But etched in the corner of her eyes and framed by straggling shocks of dark hair he could see the consequence of war and an unfair world. Beneath the calm façade of Tracy Aspen lay memories of death and the fragility of life.

He slid the stands of hair softly behind her ears. She moaned, thoughts far away in some foreign land, perhaps. He could love this woman, a woman of deep compassion and innocent resolve. There would be pain. That was life. Still he would gladly share her pains, hopefully she would share his—take it in and mold it into something more tolerable.

Wind buffeted the wood-framed window. She stirred. Despite a stack of logs roaring in the fireplace the chill of the bedroom had yet to abate. Leaving on his thermal T-shirt and slipping into wool pajamas, he eased into the bed next to her. She breathed deeply once. His side of the bed warmed quickly under the down comforter and quilt. The heat of Tracy's young body penetrated to his core and warmed him.

The tightness in his neck and back eased. As he drifted off to sleep, he sensed an animalistic urge that seemed both wrong and right at the same time. He awoke with a start. Searching amber eyes studied his face as delicate fingers traced the stubble from his ear, across his chin, and ended on his lower lip.

"What?" he said.

"What, what?" she replied.

He looked over her shoulder at the digital clock on the bedside stand, 3:05 AM. She smiled but did not take her finger off his lower lip. Instead she slowly massaged it back and forth.

"With all the chewing this lip gets I'd of thought it would be worse for the wear." She wrinkled her nose at him mischievously.

"Normally it gets very little attention," he said, then used his tongue to fence with her fingers. "Lately it has had a lot of challenges to deal with."

"Oh! Me or a nuclear holocaust?"

He felt a chapped tightness in his lips as a chuckle escaped. He took her hand and kissed the cool softness.

"Tell me something," she said. "Is there anything about you and the militia I should know?" She held his gaze without wavering.

She wanted answers before going any further with him.

"No! Honestly, I've never even talked with any of those lunatics." The base of his neck tightened. "Some of the guys in college and their families were probably involved ... I never asked."

"Okay. So, what happened with the Park Service?" She pushed a lock of his hair off his forehead. Apparently she wanted all the answers. At least she was asking. Natalie had never even done that.

A tingling sprang from his stomach up through his spine. "It was my fault."

"That's obviously what the Internal Affairs people thought. What really happened?"

He continued to hold her hand and she continued to stare at him.

"I was the senior ranger on site." Jake shook his head. "Procedures weren't followed and someone had to be held responsible."

"The incident where Bret Peterson died."

Jake's stomach soured. He swallowed hard. "We were on a search and rescue assignment for lost hikers on the backside of the monument." He sat up on his elbow. "The Service was short-handed and we left in a hurry because it was getting dark. I had my climbing gear but Bret had left his in his apartment."

"Bret was the guy from Texas who had just moved up?"

"Yeah, a last minute reassignment and first time in the snow and ice."

Tracy breathed deeply and rubbed her hand on his chest. She moved her face closer to his. "And he fell."

Jake nodded. "Two of the hikers had decided to climb the cliff east of Horse Thief Ridge. The rocks were icy and we only had my equipment." He again picked up Tracy's hand. She wrapped her other hand around his and massaged the tightness from his palm. He breathed deeply, relaxation spreading up his arm into his shoulders and back. An urge to lean forward and taste her moist lips overwhelmed him.

Her tongue subtly moistened her lips as he fought for concentration.

"I left Peterson posted at the top of the cliff to assist if anyone needed immediate evacuation, and I free-hand climbed down with a rescue line. It was a moderately technical climb, especially with the ice, even so I reached the two without much trouble ... neither of them were injured and I fashioned a sling to prevent them from falling." His pulse bounded in his throat like the day he'd explained the accident to the investigation board.

Tracy eased closer and put her arm over his shoulder.

"My intent was to contact the Ranger station and get a climbing rescue team sent out. It wasn't that cold. Those guys would have been fine all night on the side of the cliff if necessary."

"And they got rescued, right?" Tracy brushed her hand through his hair. Understanding, love and acceptance coursed down his spine at her touch, magical and anointing.

He twisted his neck further, relieving the tension. "Yeah, they came out of everything fine. Both of them testified at the hearing. Really, it had all gone perfect until Bret decided to try climbing down to us without someone to tend him ... I'd told him to stay up on the rim." Jake's throat tightened. "Maybe I should have been more explicit in my instructions." He swallowed hard but it took him two tries to actually swallow. "The next thing I knew I heard a grunt and stone and dirt showered down on us—I was busy tying a line through one of the men's backpack and didn't see anything."

Tracy lay her cheek softly against his chest. He was sucking deep wrenching breaths, as if he were crouched on the side of the cliff all over again.

"The older of the two men said someone had fallen from the top of the cliff ... At first I thought it was one of the hikers. But then Bret would not answer my calls." Jake closed his eyes and for the thousandth time wished the accident to go away. "I climbed down to the ravine and found him badly injured. He wasn't breathing and only had a weak slow pulse. I did individual CPR for over half an hour."

A tear ran down Tracy's cheek.

"He'd hit his head on the way down ... It was pretty clear he wasn't going to make it."

She lay with her arms around him for a long time—and sniffled as more tears escaped, falling on his shirt. "Thanks for telling me. I'm sorry you had to go through that."

"I'm sure it was nothing like what you went through the last few years."

She sighed deeply and held him more tightly. He delicately stroked her hair. They said nothing for a long time.

Eventually he pulled away, unsure if she was sleeping again or still awake. He crept out of the bedroom noticing the clock at 3:52 AM, closed the door, and slipped down the stairs.

Yang slept fitfully with two foul-weather coats draped over his chest and legs. Duke's tail thumped four times. Outside the Tahoe's exhaust curled across the ranch yard before disappearing into the dark, aided by the relentless northwest wind.

•

Running water with the occasional splash echoed under the door to the bedroom. Jake's bedroom and she was in Jake's bed. With Jake last night. Tracy pulled the covers up to her neck and stared at the ceiling. The musky scent of maleness still hung over the sheets. She buried her face in the pillow next to her. A soapy freshness with a slight tinge of oak teased her and brought a warmth to her chest, abdomen, and lower. Jake.

And just like that she knew that she wanted nothing more than to live in Palmer in this house with him and have his children. She just needed to get rid of the nuclear bomb first.

She threw off the covers, slipped the door open, and pushed into the steamy bathroom. Behind the shower curtain Jake hummed a Christmas song as he scrubbed his hair.

Tracy quietly removed her clothing, eased back the curtain, and stepped in behind a surprised cowboy. "Need a little help in here?"

"Well, since you're here." He handed her a bar of soap. She spooned from behind, the tightness of Jake's buttocks pushed against her naked abdomen tingling her skin. She placed a generous lather on his chest and continued down to his abdomen and thighs.

He turned around and positioned his powerful body and aroused manhood against her. She pulled his head down, kissed him hungrily, and nibbled on his irresistible lower lip. It was every bit as amazing as she'd always imagined. Her heart pounded. "I love you, Jake Moran."

Cradling her with a hand on her back and one resting on her naked right buttock he stared deep into her eyes. "I love you, too, Tracy Aspen."

Her warmth and wetness ground against his excited loin. His jaw lifted with a moan. "I've waited ten years for this, Jake ... and I'm not waiting another day."

He smiled down at her. She wrapped her arms around his neck and mounted the grinning cowboy. His lower lip quivered. Then, she was pinned against the back of the shower. He tenderly began a loving attack on her womanhood that lived up to every expectation of the past ten years.

She lay her head on his chest, warm water plastered hair against her cheek and his chest. She wished the moment would never end. "Merry Christmas," he said through water cascading across his face and onto her chest.

"That's right, Merry Christmas." She chuckled throatily. "Hey, do you think we can get back into town tonight for the pageant?"

"Possibly." He rubbed his chin. "Depends on how much the county is able to clear the road from Palmer or if we can follow the Air Force guys' tracks back out to the gate."

Tracy shivered and huddled against Jake's warm body.

He reached behind her and turned off the cooling shower water. "End of hot water," he said. "But I do have coffee brewing downstairs."

He handed her a towel and fished another one out of a basket next to the sink. They wrapped themselves in the towels and Jake pulled her close in an embrace that felt as natural as Christmas.

"You know, I hate to tell you this," Jake said seriously. "I think someone stole the baby Jesus from the church nativity scene."

Tracy patted water from his back, not quite sure what he was talking about. "You mean last year?"

"No, this year. When we went by the other day all the wise men, Mary and Joseph, along with the animals were all there ... including the manger. But no baby Jesus." He rubbed his hand across her shoulder and played with the wet ends of her hair.

"You know." She smiled. "I'll bet if we get to the church tonight for Christmas service, the baby Jesus will be back."

"You really think so?" The fine wrinkles at the edge of his eyes scrunched into a frown.

"Trust me on this one," she said as the grinding growl of heavy military trucks drifted up from the ranch yard.

•

Jake kissed Tracy on the nose, his chest swelling like a balloon about to burst. "We'd better get dressed. The cavalry has arrived."

He grabbed fresh underwear, jeans, and a Carhartt work shirt. Tracy pulled her meager selection out of her backpack. "Sorry." She frowned as she held up the Arizona State sweats she'd slept in.

Jake shrugged and grabbed his coat. A cell phone fell out on the floor and Tracy, still in underpants and bra, bent and picked it up. Her head tilted and her lips tightened. "This isn't yours."

"No, man I completely forgot about that." Jake leaned next to her bare shoulder. Her near naked body and alluring fragrance threatening to reignite his arousal.

Her knitted brows stared at him.

"What?" He said.

"This is one of those throw-away cell phones you buy at Walmart or in a drug store."

"It's Carl Atwood's," Jake said. "It fell out of his coat when we rolled him over up on the mountain."

"It's like the burner cell phones we found on insurgents in Afghanistan. They use them a few days, week at the most, and then toss them in a fire. Any link to them cut." She turned the phone over and pointed. "It still has the store's bar code on it."

Jake slid into his coat as closing doors could be heard in the ranch yard.

Tracy made no move to put on more clothes. She glanced from the phone to Jake.

It was starting to add up. Why would Carl Atwood have a second cell phone? Probably one that could not be traced back to him. Why had the Spearfish Canyon disappearances never been solved? And, what was Bret Peterson really doing assigned to Mount Rushmore? That was just the start of the questions.

Jake took the phone from Tracy and activated the message screen. He selected recent messages and found mundane queries regarding restaurants and movie theatres all with 605 area codes, South Dakota. He was about to change to recent telephone calls when Tracy pointed to the bottom of the screen.

"There's another number at the bottom," she said.

Jake scrolled down to the number which had no text associated with it.

Tracy tapped her lip. "He must have erased that text."

"What do you mean?"

"For the number to be there, it means that texting was done either to the number or from the number ... and if there's no text associated with the number then it must have been erased."

She picked up her iPhone and began dialing the number 1-416-596-0575. The preceding one indicated an international number. She put the phone on speaker as they listened.

"Thank you for calling the Toronto Islamic Center. The center is open from—"

Tracy pushed end, one eyebrow raised she glance out the window.

"He shot at me," Jake said, a hot poker pushing into the base of his neck.

Tracy wheeled around. "Atwood shot at you?"

"During the shooting on the ridge," Jake said. "At first I thought it was just a stray shot ... you know, when he was grazed on the head."

Tracy began quickly dressing. "This is not good. Is he a dirty agent ... a mole?"

"I don't know. But I'll tell you this, he shot at me from the back, while the bullets were flying, and just missed."

Tracy stared up at him.

"And, more often than not, Atwood has been the common factor in my problems with the Service and the unsolved occurrences we've had over the past few years." Jake rubbed his neck. "It all starts to add up."

"Do you think McAllister or the Homeland guys are in on it?" Tracy asked.

"I don't think so ... McAllister has no reason to be in South

Dakota or have any dealings with the Park Service unless the President's travel comes into play." Jake paced back and forth. "Do we have enough evidence to go to her or the Homeland guys?"

"She's already told me that the Secret Service knows there was a leak of the President's schedule." Tracy stepped in front of Jake and took his hands in hers. "She is technically the agent in charge."

"You think she'll listen to us ... believe us?"

"I don't know," Tracy said shaking her head. "But what other options do we have?"

Jake bit on his lower lip. "None. You ready to go? It'll probably go better coming from both of us."

She smiled, and standing on tip-toes, kissed him firmly on the lips.

Chapter 23

Pre-Dawn Christmas Morning, Moran Ranch

The sight of military personnel, large duce-and-a-half trucks, and a bomb-disposal armored-vehicle propelled Tracy back to the Gulf War. She breathed deeply the frosty Dakota winter-air and willed the beating of her chest to calm.

"I could use a warm shower," Atwood said pointing to the condensation covered window in the second-floor gable of the ranch house. "You two leave any hot water?" His eyes wandered up and down Tracy.

"We were hoping you guys wouldn't be around here much longer," Jake said.

A Colonel had directed a burly non-com with dirty fingernails, to back Jake's truck up to the rear of the demolition team's tracked vehicle. The armor wouldn't give any protection against a detonating nuclear device.

Two field medics and a trauma physician's assistant stabilized Yang's leg and gingerly slid him into a troop-transport vehicle. He smiled and gave Tracy a thumbs up. Duke stood, paws on the front window, dutifully observing all the goings on.

"Jake said the two of you wanted to talk." McAllister rounded the back of the SUV, hair and coat perfectly arranged. Crawford stood with his foot on the running board talking to Atwood through the window.

"Maybe in the house," Tracy said. "The coffee Jake put on should be finished by now."

McAllister surveyed the ranch yard and nodded. Busy soldiers, accentuated by the yard and vehicle lights, moved in and out of the snow flurries. They went about their morning like it was just another day at the potential nuclear holocaust.

Despite talking with Crawford, Atwood's head turned as she and McAllister entered the house.

"How's it going out there?" Jake asked as the women removed their coats. They left their boots on, as the wood floor was already awash in dirt and snow from the many intrusions. The Colonel in charge had just stepped out ahead of them.

"We should be out of your hair within the hour." McAllister accepted a mason jar of coffee from Jake and held it appreciatively in both hands. The tiny crow's feet at the corners of her eyes now had a few forehead wrinkles as company.

"What's up?" McAllister was not one for small talk.

Jake nodded to Tracy.

"We may have some information on your itinerary leak ... or it might just be incidental intel." Tracy withdrew Atwood's cellphone from her pocket and handed it to McAllister.

She turned it over twice. "We think the leak came from the Canadian end," McAllister said. "I already told you that."

"This cell phone has evidence of text messaging to the Islamic Center in Toronto." Tracy's pulse accelerated. Sweet pine scent arose from a Christmas candle burning on the sideboard. She smiled at Jake and took his hand. "It fell out of Carl Atwood's coat during the shooting up on the ridge."

"Does he know he lost it?" McAllister asked.

"He's probably figured that out by now," Jake answered. "But he was unconscious when I picked it up and may think it's lost somewhere between here and the Monument."

"There's more," Tracy glanced through the window to the ranch yard. "Jake thinks Atwood tried to shoot him just before he was grazed."

"Really!" McAllister sat back in her chair, tapping her index finger on the Mason jar.

Jake squeezed Tracy's hand.

Finally McAllister spoke. "Obviously you both understand what you're inferring." She glanced repeatedly between the two of them. "Honestly it doesn't make a lot of sense."

Jake stood and walked to the front window. Duke joined him and sat obediently next to him as Jake stared at the military invasion of his property. "I've had other run-ins with Atwood, Agent." He drank a big gulp of coffee. "And if you look at the record, on paper, I'm probably not the best source."

"So what are you trying to say?" McAllister studied Jake sternly.

"I think if you ever get to the bottom of this you'll find it has to do with drugs or money or both."

McAllister rubbed her lips thoughtfully. "Look, let's let him think for now that his extra cell phone is safely lost on the mountainside under three feet of snow." She crooked her head at Tracy. "And, we'll keep this under the purview of Presidential Secret Service until we get it ferreted out."

"That's all we're asking for," Jake said.

It was going to get swept under the rug. Tracy's ears burned.

The agent rolled her eyes. "You know that if anything turns up on this ... you likely won't hear a word about it. The FBI is not about to publicly announce any treason in the ranks, unless they are forced to."

"If Carl Atwood doesn't end up being the head of the Sioux Falls FBI office, I think I'll have my answer." Jake said.

McAllister pointed at Jake. "Sorry for ruining your Christmas." She finished the coffee and walked carefully across the slippery floor to the front door. Before leaving she turned to the two of them. "Merry Christmas and thanks."

•

According to her iPhone, it was after sunrise when the bomb and military convoy finally left the ranch. You couldn't tell with the dark cloud cover, snow, and blowing drifts. The headlights of Jake's pickup and the Air Force duce-and-a-halves barely penetrated the curtain of Canadian snow.

She sat next to Jake while Duke covered the passenger's seat, head lounging on Tracy's leg. With the back window, rifle rack, and his .270 adding to the rattle of the truck, she felt like she was in a country song. Crawling along at under thirty miles-per-hour she figured just short of an hour to get to Jake's mom's house. She could walk to the church for the pageant, if it even happened.

She fiddled with the truck radio, new just three years ago according to Jake, FM 101.3, continuous Christmas songs since

Thanksgiving. Snow apparently had no effect on radio-waves, as *Little Drummer Boy* replaced Bing Crosby's *White Christmas*.

"I feel so stupid." She shook her head and raised the loaf of bread in her lap. "We're bringing bread to your mom's and sister's Christmas Dinner!" She petted Duke. "It isn't even homemade."

Jake bit down on his lip. "They'll understand."

"Hey, they might understand you bringing Sunbeam Honey Wheat bread to Christmas Dinner. But Catherine will never let me live this down."

Jake chuckled despite trying to keep a straight face.

"It's not like I'm very domestic with cooking and all." Her chest tightened. "But at least I could have tried."

Jake patted the hand holding on to the precious package of bread. "Maybe it will help if I explain that you were too busy ferreting out double-agents and saving the western United States from nuclear holocaust."

"Yeah, that might work once … but not for next Christmas." She laughed. "I better learn to cook—at least mashed potatoes."

• • •

Rory Church

Rory Church is a writer of romance and inspirational fiction. He is a long-time Gulf Coast resident and member of Romance Writers of America. Rory is a Naval Academy graduate and military veteran. He lives and travels with his wife and high school sweetheart, who is the romantic soul and critical center of his writing. He continues to write overlooking the emerald waters of the Gulf of Mexico or while pondering the stream outside his cabin in the western North Carolina Mountains. He says, "Inspiration comes from many corners and the trail of life often leads to curves and drop-offs never expected. But it yields the pebbles and roots of which great stories are made."

You might also enjoy . . .

Special Forces operative Morgan Raush rarely speaks to the handsome, blue-eyed Russian agent, Dmitry Rurik, about anything except military business if she can help it. They've formed an uneasy alliance during their joint mission in remote Uzbekistan. But now, through a twist of fate, the two must depend on one another to survive rugged mountains, blizzards and enemy attacks.

In the midst of icy nights and glowing fires, Morgan discovers Dmitry is much more than she'd first thought—a man torn between two ideologies, a man driven by faith and family. Then again, maybe the spy is only telling her what he wants her to believe? Morgan has only five days left to sort out the conflict in her heart, and only five days left ... to make it home by Christmas.